ORBITS

ALSO BY JEREMY SCOTT

ORBITS

THE ABLES
BOOK FOUR

JEREMY SCOTT

TURNER
PUBLISHING COMPANY

Turner Publishing Company
Nashville, Tennessee
www.turnerpublishing.com

Orbits: The Ables, Book IV

Cover art and design by Phil Huling
Book design by William Ruoto

Library of Congress Cataloging-in-Publication Data
  Names: Scott, Jeremy (Writer on cinema), author.
  Title: Orbits / Jeremy Scott.
  Description: Nashville, Tennessee : Turner Publishing, [2022] | Series: The
    Ables, 16844233 ; Book IV
  Identifiers: LCCN 2022001407 (print) | LCCN 2022001408 (ebook) | ISBN
    9781684423453 (paperback) | ISBN 9781684423460 (hardcover) | ISBN
    9781684423477 (ebook)
  Subjects: CYAC: Ability—Fiction. | Superheroes—Fiction. |
    Diseases—Fiction. | LCGFT: Novels.
  Classification: LCC PZ7.1.S336845 Or 2022 (print) | LCC PZ7.1.S336845
    (ebook) | DDC 372.4—dc24/eng/20220521
  LC record available at https://lccn.loc.gov/2022001407
  LC ebook record available at https://lccn.loc.gov/2022001408

Printed in the United States of America

"HEROES OF THIS WILDLY INVENTIVE AND
UNPREDICTABLE SUPERHERO EPIC DON'T WANT TO
BE IGNORED, OR PITIED, OR PLACED ON A PEDESTAL.
THEY WANT WHAT ALL OF US WANT: THE CHANCE TO
FORGE THEIR OWN DESTINY. THE FICTIONAL WORLD
OF THE ABLES STRUGGLES TO ADMIT IT NEEDS ITS
TEAM OF SPECIAL ED HEROES. BUT IT DOES, AND I
WOULD SAY OUR POP CULTURE LANDSCAPE (AND, YOU
KNOW, YOUR BOOKSHELF) NEEDS THEM EVEN MORE."

—JASON PARGIN, *NEW YORK TIMES* BESTSELLING
AUTHOR OF *IF THIS BOOK EXISTS, YOU'RE IN THE
WRONG UNIVERSE*

MOST OF THIS STORY IS TOLD FROM MY OWN PERSPECTIVE, BUT SOME EVENTS WERE RELAYED TO ME IN DETAIL BY CLOSE FRIENDS AND FAMILY AFTER THE FACT.

1

STARS

The stars were lovely tonight.

There were many times I took my newfound sight for granted. But starry nights were not among them.

I was no longer blind. Science had finally created an artificial eye implant, and I was one of the first one hundred to undergo the procedure. That alone made me feel entitled, though the truth was that the procedure had been entirely developed by custodian scientists, and we'd yet to share the treatment with the general public because . . . well . . . the general public wanted us dead.

Most of us *were* dead.

Anyway, having sight was nice. It was everything I'd always dreamed it would be. I was no longer hindered by my body's inadequacies. I was fully capable as a human. Beyond that, I was even more capable than most humans, as my implanted eyes came with thermal vision, infrared, and night vision capabilities. I could even save video of what I was seeing and download it to a computer, though I'd yet to make use of that talent.

But I was still unsettled.

I snapped myself out of my stargazing.

"Winnie, when was Pluto's designation changed from planet to dwarf planet and why?" I said, much the same way some parents say "Did you finish your homework?"

"Two thousand five," she began, before correcting herself. "No, two thousand six. And the designation was changed because of the discovery of several other bodies in the Kuiper Belt that were the same size as Pluto."

"That is correct! Good job. Alright, Hen," I said loudly, just before chopping another piece of wood with a metallic thud. "Most influential invention of all time. Go."

Hen was short for Henry, and he was my youngest child at twelve years old.

"Johannes Gutenberg," Henry replied instantly. "Inventor of the printing press. The ability for newspapers, magazines, and other publications to rapidly print many copies at once drastically changed the flow of information and the power of those who held it." I heard him shuffle down the line in our backyard garden, harvesting greens and veggies as he went.

"Acceptable answer," I said, loading up another chunk of wood to slice. "Winnie?"

"It's so obvious that it's Alexander Graham Bell that it's not even funny. Communication over long distances in real time? That's relevant even today! Whereas Henry's newspapers are dying left and right, most of them dead already." Her voice came from several yards into the orchard, where she was harvesting apples.

I liked to combine schoolwork with chores. It worked the body and the mind, and it ultimately gave the kids more free time in the late evenings to do their own thing.

Winnie, fourteen years old, was short for Winnifred, the first name of the most important schoolteacher I'd ever had, Mrs. Crouch.

My Winnie was as impatient as she was whip-smart. She was enough like her mother to make it hard for me sometimes, and then the rest of her was more like her uncle Patrick—quick, fiery, energetic. She was a handful, and she was more precious to me than almost anything.

"Rebuttal," I barked.

Henry was ready. "Just because print journalism is dying in the modern world doesn't negate the original invention's importance. That's like saying that the Beatles' influence dies if and when the government outlaws rock and roll. The printing press gave birth to journalism in America, which is still alive and well, despite having moved from print to radio and TV to the internet, and then back to radio after the Liquidation."

Henry was named for my late best friend, whom we'd lost in battle in Washington, DC, back when we were still teenagers. I was ultimately both glad and regretful that I had given my son the name. It served as a constant reminder of what I considered one of my biggest failures, but my friend Henry's actions there also ensured his name would never mean anything short of "hero."

The kids and I had most everything we needed right here, I repeatedly told myself.

A nearby stream provided water that we boiled to purify. We had a garden for vegetables and greens. Wild boar, fish from the stream, and venison from wild deer made up most of our protein diet. We had a small smokehouse to cure some of the meat.

We had chickens and rabbits we tended as well, providing us with eggs and even more options for meat.

Besides, the kids had never known anything other than this, I constantly reminded myself. They'd never known central heat and air, cable television, or email. They were so young when I'd moved us out here, they'd grown up thinking our kind of remote farm/cabin living was the norm. Or, at least, I hoped that they had.

The only time we needed to go to town was for gasoline to power the truck, the mower, and the generators—and to stock up on feed and other small-farm basics. And look, "town" these days was a pretty limited description. Depending on which direction we drove, there was one general store still open, one bank and one bar at most . . . a general store at the very least.

Most everything had closed—not only here, but everywhere.

Everyone was scared. Everyone was wary. Shop owners looked you over more, and some began locking up their merchandise behind padlocked gates.

I'd been here with the kids for a decade, so the locals knew me and continued to sell to me, even if some adopted clandestine methods of exchanging product for payment.

Our cottage was mostly solar powered, and when the sun refused to cooperate there were two waterwheels in the stream that provided backup power—while also serving as mills, providing us with flour and cornmeal.

Beyond all that, we also had a three-year supply of canned goods.

Short of an apocalypse, we were set to withstand most any event. And these days, there were some wild rumors about coming catastrophes.

"Victory to Henry this round," I said as I heard my daughter groan. "Alright, Win, your turn."

"I'm almost done," she replied, dumping a few more apples into her basket. "Give me something easy." She smiled and leaped back up into the nearest tree.

"Paul Revere was not the only rider who—"

"William Dawes, Samuel Prescott, and Israel Bissell," she replied confidently, racing over to my location on the back porch to set down her basket of apples for approval.

I looked down at the basket, then back up at my daughter. "I think you're getting faster by the day."

Winnie was gifted with super speed, just like her favorite uncle, Patrick. Of course, she'd only met Patrick a few times, but those visits had left a lasting impression. There was a strong bond between custodians that shared the same power. Winnifred talked most, above all other subjects, about reuniting with her uncle Patrick. After that it was boys. I wasn't a fan of either topic, but I definitely preferred talking about her uncle.

"Can I be dismissed now?" she asked.

"Indeed," I agreed.

She dashed off to her room.

Henry's power was laser-based, and I'd never seen anything quite like it. He typically shot lasers from his palms, but rather than being offensive weapons, those lasers were used like force fields, pushing back against a target, but also sometimes enveloping a target momentarily, as though defending it from harm.

He was still young; his powers were still manifesting. But for now, his abilities seemed defensive in nature. It bothered him like you couldn't imagine. He wanted to be offensive and brutishly strong, like most boys would.

Since I'd gone off the grid when the kids were quite young, I'd had years to debate whether or not to tell them about their powers. And if so, exactly what to tell them. I'd settled on a slightly modified version of the truth:

You have superpowers, because I do and your late mother did. She died in an explosion fighting against the very man who now wants to wipe out ALL those with powers. Which is why we live here in the woods, in secret.

Outside the cottage, our family owned several acres of unoccupied forest all around us in every direction, allowing for excellent exploration, education, and even hunting and fishing. The kids and I could run and yell and enjoy this nature around us with relative assurance that we would never be discovered.

Sure, there were custodian-seeking satellites, so we heard. But those were on a schedule we could follow. And the rumored drones would be caught by our motion sensors miles before they got to our cabin, which had a camouflage roof we could set up in thirty seconds.

Inside, there were limited resources for my children to explore their youth and their superpowers. Physical space was the biggest limitation, as it turned out. Our cabin had three bedrooms, but only one and a half floors, so all the bedrooms were in earshot of one another. If one of us snored or had a nightmare, we'd all hear it.

Entertainment was also mostly an outdoors activity.

We owned a bunch of tapes and discs of movies and shows from my youth and even my adulthood. Somehow, despite the odds, we even had an ancient VCR and most of the other media players necessary to view old and new films and home movies.

Our televisions were capable of receiving signals, but no one on the network side of things—at least none of the privately owned stations—was sending anything out except the constant "turn yourself in" of the State Superintendent's "promos." The State's channel itself churned out regular news, but almost none of it was to be trusted.

I had hardwired our family TV to convert these signals into static. I didn't want my kids hearing about it and I didn't want to hear about it myself. I'd gone years without a panic attack, and I knew my triggers . . . I wasn't about to induce a new one out of raw curiosity.

In hindsight, it was probably a mistake to ignore the state broadcasts for as long as I did.

Anyway, a few private pirate broadcasts did exist, and the kids liked to

sneak their tiny radios very late at night to listen to the news outside the parameters I had set for them. I knew I couldn't stop them from fully learning
about the outside world forever, so I was willing to let them explore as they
got older.

The sober truth was that I actually needed to tell them about the outside
world, because the outside world wanted them dead. Soon they would be
using their powers to defend themselves instead of racing apples and other
various produce over to me from the gardens for inspection.

Henry was cooking tonight, and the spices were so heavy in the air my eyes
started watering from the smell alone. Henry was a fan of heat.

Each night, we took turns choosing the menu and serving as head chef, and
both kids had been cooking with me since they were old enough to read a recipe,
so we ate pretty well. Of course, because they were kids, they had their moments
as picky eaters. They each had meals they loved to prepare and eat that the other
couldn't stand. So we had to make exceptions and put limits in place.

Tonight, Henry was making a dish he called Menacin' Venison—he
liked giving all his dishes catchy names. It was an incredibly spicy meal com-
prised of deer meat that had been slow-roasted over the fire then pulled with
a fork like barbeque. He usually served it with some no-knead campfire bread
or cornbread and some kind of beans—tonight it was white beans.

The bread and the beans were the only mercy on the plate. I often wondered how Em and I had managed to create a human being that enjoyed fiery
flavors, since she and I had had such mild palates.

"Smells like you overdid it this time, son," I said as I scooted back
my chair and sat down at the table. Winnie was already seated, eyes buried in one of those books about the precocious redheaded Canadian girl.
It was her favorite series of books. The girl loved to read. She loved it so
much I ached that we had such a small library and such limited access
to new books.

New books weren't being printed, outside the government propaganda
stuff. Underground books existed too, here and there, but nothing that our

general store would ever carry. We were stuck with the books I'd brought along when I moved us here in the dead of night. I'd left so many books behind . . . I had left so many things behind.

"I concur," Winnifred said, agreeing with my assessment of Henry's heavy spice hand.

"Well, maybe if you let me serve it more than once a month," Hen said over his shoulder from the stove, "I wouldn't get so excited and overdo it."

"You're saying," I said playfully, "in order to avoid double spicy food once a month, I need to let you cook regular spicy food once a week?"

"Exactly," he replied just as the venison left his spatula and landed on my plate. "Some for you, Father," he said as he then moved down the table to the other end. "Some for you, dear sister," he said with a false sincerity. "And some for me," he declared as he dumped the entire remaining batch of meat onto his own plate.

I bent a little lower and smelled the venison. For a half second, I smiled, because there was a clear savory smell there, but then it was overpowered by the spices and herbs Henry had used to turn up the heat. My head went back faster than if I'd been punched. I immediately looked up at Winnie, only to see a similar expression on her face.

"To my credit," Henry said, returning to the table with a dish in each hand, "I have provided you tonight with more options than normal for cleansing and cooling that palate. We have these biscuits here, and some really nice mashed potatoes with *zero* seasoning." He looked at me and winked before rushing back to the stove. "And finally, these white beans, which have no added heat beyond salt and pepper."

I couldn't help but beam. My kids were still so young, but so old. So mature. So capable. Sure, I was going to live with the spice level of this meal for the next twenty-four hours in various ways, but I would do so smiling, because I loved my son.

Winnifred started loading up her plate with beans and biscuits as Henry dumped hot sauce on his venison.

"I think we're forgetting something," I said with a smile. "Henry's turn to cook means it's . . . Dad's turn to pick the music!"

Both kids groaned.

As with the books, our music library was limited. We had about fifty records, twenty or so cassette tapes, and maybe a hundred CDs. Almost all of it was mine or Em's, and the kids' tastes in music had been limited to what they liked best of their parents' collection. There were radio stations, of course, but all the stations available were under the control of the government, which mostly meant that only the plainest, most watered-down songs ever got played, and those were interspersed with propaganda ads.

Left to my own desires, I preferred jazz. I liked the spontaneity, the improvisation, and the feeling that the music could go anywhere at any moment in any song. The kids hated jazz, and had each carved out about half their mother's music library to call their own.

Henry had all the stuff Em liked in high school and college, when we'd met and first fallen in love. That was mostly indie music; rock, but with harmonies and also some angst.

Winnie liked the music Em had gravitated toward as an adult. This was largely show tunes and adult contemporary music—powerful songs about love and life and loss.

They groaned tonight because they feared I would pick another jazz album, as I'd done dozens of times before, sometimes only to torture them.

Instead, I made a big show of things, only to put on my favorite live orchestra recording of Vivaldi's *Four Seasons*. Both kids ceased their objections and melted into smiles of comfort at the first few notes. The only music Em and I had ever both agreed on was classical, particularly strings. Ballets, concertos, chamber music . . . we both enjoyed the soothing comfort of classical music, and had somehow passed that down to both children—perhaps the best thing our DNA had accomplished to date.

"Good choice, Dad," Winnie finally admitted as I sat back down at the table. She took a bite before waving her hand in front of her mouth. "Although to hit the nail fully on the head you should have started with 'Summer'!"

She started chugging water as Henry and I laughed, only for the heat of my own first bite to hit, and the laughter turned to tears.

We all laughed, but no one laughed longer and harder than Henry, for he

was the only one intestinally set up to endure the challenge of the Menacin'
Venison.

When both kids were inside for the night I went out to the front porch with
Monster and lit a cigar, easing into the rocker. I puffed and rocked and enjoyed the sounds of the natural world around me—the bugs, the frogs, the
nocturnal animals. I had eyesight now, but my hearing was still my strongest
natural sense.

Still, my sight was wonderful and wondrous to me. Every flash of every lightning bug was special. Every trail of every meteor meant something.
Hell, even looking at the moon was magical.

Monster, our German shepherd, seemed to hear every sound, his ears
making micro-adjustments for each noise from the forest.

I looked up and gaped at the stars and the faint view of the Milky Way.
I'd never given light pollution its due as a villain to science and wonder. Up
here, away from any kind of major city, and after so many cities had been
leveled . . . we had a view I'd never even realized existed.

City lights be damned; I was in awe of the light show above.

I closed my eyes, content to drift off to sleep right here in the chair, feeling no anxiety, no depression, and no sense of panic whatsoever.

I may never have been more at ease.

2

LAST TRIP INTO TOWN

Monster loved riding in the back of the pickup, and I usually let Winnie ride back there with him if she wanted to. I know it's technically not safe, but she and that dog had a special bond and I had a hard time saying no when they ganged up on me.

We were low on enough supplies that it was time to take another trip to town. And for the first time I wished I'd been keeping up with the news better. I guess I thought that as long as we stayed way off the grid, the real news would never impact us. But I was wrong.

St. Valley looked empty.

It was the nearest town and our trusted destination for supplies every other month, but something was different this time.

The lights were off at the bank, the bar, the "recreation" house, the hotel, and the tailor.

It was like a ghost town.

A few cars were abandoned in odd places here and there. The only thing missing to complete the picture was a tumbleweed.

The general store had faint lights on, and it drew us in like insects to a flame. We placed our faces up against the glass windows, cupping our hands around our eyes to provide shade, only to have Zip Thomeson, the owner, shock us all nearly to death by popping out of the front door with a hearty "Hello!"

While we all reeled in our own way, Zip continued without missing a beat. "I was starting to think I wouldn't see you guys again before shutting down."

"Why are you shutting down?" I asked, even as the kids ran inside and grabbed a shopping cart.

"No customers. You're the first I've had in more than a week. But beyond that . . . no suppliers. No one's delivering here anymore. Just to stay open I'd have to contact and set up deals with thirty or forty independent suppliers, and even then those federal zealots would find them and shut them down. They're trying to wear us all out, I'm afraid. Grind us down to nothing."

"I'm sorry," I said, honestly. "Is there anything I can do, outside of making a huge final purchase here and now?"

"No," he laughed. "You're kind to ask. The wife and I are all set up for at least five to ten years halfway up the mountain here behind me. I just wish I could keep supplying the likes of you."

The authorities, in their pursuit of custodians, were going after any and all possible suppliers, hoping to cut off these remote heroes and force them back into the light. Supposedly they had some kind of ledger—a master list of custodians provided by those they'd captured and tortured thus far. And they wouldn't rest until they crossed every name off the list.

It just might work. Or not.

They'd already killed so many custodians. And a great many of the non-superpowered humans in North America as well. One might even wonder who they were trying to protect from whom since the arrests and killings had been so indiscriminate.

We spent every cent of cash that we had, or at least we tried to. Zip insisted on leaving us with $500 for our own future adventures. The rest of our savings went to he and his wife and their hopeful future in the caves above.

In exchange, we had free run of the store. Zip said we'd been so loyal and were leaving him with such a huge final payday, we could take anything and everything we could fit in the truck.

We had so much of our own food supply back at the cabin in one way or another, so we spent most of our truck space on feed, seed, and gasoline. We also grabbed a bunch of underwear and socks—because we were seasoned outdoorspeople that knew the importance of underwear and socks—as well as a chunk of his stock of long-lasting proteins: mostly cured meats, jerky, smoked salmon, and some nuts.

He repeatedly assured us that these items would be stolen or looted soon anyway, so he was happy to see them go to us. But it still felt a little wrong to be looting with permission.

We piled the truck so full that Henry had to sit on his big sister's lap on the drive home, which you can be sure he enjoyed, as any twelve-year-old boy would.

We would be set for many months now. And beyond that . . . we were just going to have to figure it out as we went. But for the near future, we were set.

The drive home was ebullient and joyous as we sang happy songs while hauling our near-future livelihood home.

I noticed fewer cars on the road than usual, and more drones overhead than usual, but we lost sight of all that once we hit the Birch Mountains Wildland Provincial Park.

We lived alongside the park. I'd intentionally built our cabin right on the property line so we'd be as surrounded by woods as possible.

It was illegal to hunt in the park, and, for now, that included the use of drones.

Our location was better than the Batcave. No one would find us here who didn't already know this is where we were.

We'd arrived home and unpacked most of the haul from Zip's before a far-off sedan crept down our dirt driveway, slowly . . . as though not to alarm us, I suppose, but it also wasn't trying to hide. Our driveway, such as it was—a dirt path connected to another dirt path—was quite long, so we saw the car coming long before it got close.

"Grab the rest of that stuff and go inside, and take the dog," I barked, and the kids obeyed, though I was quite certain they would move to the nearest open window to see and overhear whatever they could.

I stayed still, standing on the porch at the top of the stairs.

In all our years out here, we had never had a single visitor, and that had been intentional. No matter who was inside that car, I was less than pleased and bordering on panic. I hadn't used my powers in more than a decade, due to an oath I'd sworn mostly to myself, but I would literally do anything to protect my babies.

The car inched forward until stopping about fifty feet away. A single individual got out on the driver's side and walked forward to the front edge of the car.

I'd had enough mystery, so I turned on my floodlights to see . . . Bentley Crittendon.

He was older, as we all were, but there was no mistaking it was him.

I caught my breath as he waved at me, smiling. Buried memories came flooding back, many bringing hints of pain. Somehow, I summoned my inner strength and quieted my mind, and made my way down the stairs.

I stopped at the bottom of the steps, sighed, and then walked slowly toward the car. I stopped about twelve feet away. For a few beats we were both silent, just taking in the moment of this unexpected reunion.

I knew enough to know that he wasn't here for any nefarious reason. If Bentley were still a villain, he'd have wiped me out before I'd even known what hit me. He wouldn't drive slowly up my driveway with his lights on, giving me several minutes to see him coming.

So, while I was nervous, I wasn't particularly afraid. I guess you could say that I was guarded.

"The last time I saw you," I finally said quietly, "you were a villain."

Bentley smiled before taking two small steps forward—without any braces or canes, I noticed. "That's funny," he laughed. "The last time I saw you, you were a hero." He stopped in front of his car and leaned back on it casually.

"I never really got a chance to be mad at you, you know," I stated. "You disappeared after everything went down up at the cave. I've got years of built-up shouting to do at you."

"I'm sure you do, and I'm perfectly willing to endure it. I deserve it all." He seemed sincere enough. "But I'm hoping that can wait."

I looked him up and down, warily. I hadn't seen him in nearly fifteen years. He appeared to be using a kind of exoskeleton on his legs to help him walk without assistance. "Nice legs," I said, honestly impressed.

"Nice eyes," he returned. "Osiris?"

There were a few brands making artificial eyeballs these days, but Osiris was top of the line—well, they were before 75 percent of the general population got wiped out in the government's war against custodians and potential future custodians. I don't think anyone was making artificial eyes anymore.

"Yeah," I chuckled. "Paid for by the custodian conglomerate . . . just before its dismantling."

"It's not dismantled, Phillip," he replied urgently. "It's only gone underground, for obvious reasons." He stepped forward a few paces. "It's greatly depleted, but it's still alive. I'm here on behalf of the resistance, and I'm here to beg you to join us as soon as possible, because we're on the verge of permanent defeat if we don't win a victory soon."

I shook my head back and forth quickly. "No, Bentley. No. We're not going to talk about hero stuff and saving the world right now." He tried to object but I just kept talking. "Right now . . . we're going to go in and have dinner so you can meet my kids. And because I'm hungry and because my daughter is an amazing cook and also because I need more time to adjust to this shit right here. Then, assuming that goes well, we can talk about what you came here for after dinner." I walked forward and extended a hand. "Deal?"

"Deal," he smiled.

We both walked up to the cabin together, a noticeable few feet between us the whole way.

"Listen," I warned just as we reached the front door, "my kids . . . they're . . . they're aware of custodians and they know their powers. They know it's not a safe world out there. But I . . . I haven't been showing them any of the state broadcasts or even the underground ones. It's obviously a mistake and I'm going to have to correct it quickly and soon, since your showing up here means things are much worse than I thought, but just . . . don't say anything about the specifics of the world out there, okay? Let me be the one to tell them."

"Of course," he agreed immediately. "Besides, there's a lot you still need to be briefed on before even you know everything, so . . ."

For Winnie's night to cook, she'd chosen to make her signature stew. She'd actually started the roast before we'd even left to go to St. Valley, letting it cook low and slow to steep in its own juices. Most cooks would make a roast first, and serve that to their families, using the leftovers to make a stew. Not Winnie. For her, the stew itself was the star. And it was, as it always was, sensational.

"You should open a restaurant!" Bentley declared.

"Right," Winnifred replied, "and who would come to it?"

Everyone got momentarily somber as she reminded us of the state of the world in her own subtle way.

"Well, I would," Bentley said with a smile. "Just incredible food."

"Me too," I added.

"Same," Hen pitched in.

After we ate, the kids took turns asking Bentley to tell stories about what I was like when I was a kid. They were fishing for embarrassing anecdotes they could use against me as leverage, but Bentley mostly only told them harmless stuff like how I got my phone smashed my first day of superhero high school or how I'd once been given a ticket for speeding in a vehicle that didn't have a functioning engine—because I'd been using my abilities to power the car.

We all laughed a lot, and I recognized how important laughter was now and was going to be for my children's future. We laughed, of course—I'd thought we used to laugh together regularly—but Bentley's stories had us rolling in ways we maybe never had.

The isolation may have been protecting my kids from physical harm, but what was it costing them otherwise?

3

THE UPDATE

When the kids finally went to bed, it was time for Bentley and me to have the serious conversation he'd come here for. I knew from experience that we'd have to go back outside to talk, or else the kids would hear every word.

It was a brisk early-fall evening, so we chose to sit in his car and talk, with the windows down a bit to keep the air circulating.

"How up-to-date are you with custodian underground news?" he asked.

"Assume I know nothing."

He paused and cocked his head. "Nothing?"

"Nothing since my wife was killed," I said, putting a finite date on things.

Milliken's warpath had taken the life of my wife, Emmaline, my children's mother. Before my very eyes on a battlefield in Baltimore, she'd teleported directly beside the villain in what she thought was a moment of weakness . . .

Bentley paused for a very long time. "That's just it," he said softly. "I have reason to believe your wife may not have died in that battle."

Without using any powers, I grabbed him by the throat and pressed his head against the glass of his driver's side window. "Do *not* go about rewriting my wife's history lightly," I growled. I had no specific reasons to trust him. This was someone who, at last glance, had utterly and completely betrayed my trust.

"He killed many foes, of course," Bentley coughed, my grip loosened but not gone. "But there are rumors that he also quietly built an arsenal of custodians for his own future use . . . for when he finds the Amplifier—the once-a-millennium hero who can take any custodian's power and amplify it by as much as a factor of fifty."

I relaxed my grasp. My breathing slowed a bit, but my guard was still up.

Bentley continued. "I believe Emmaline is part of this group, and . . . more importantly. . . I believe we need her help to save my son." He paused for a good several seconds. "My son."

So those were the stakes. My old friend-turned-villain-turned-hero was asking me to help save his son, dangling the prospect that I might see my wife again at some point.

I withdrew my hand. It seemed too good to be true.

"Your son?"

We'd sent spies into the state prisons, hoping to find evidence of the survival of our friends, but we'd always come up empty.

The only survivor of the blast that killed Em seemed to be the State Superintendent himself. We were left to mourn the rest.

And from that day forward I vowed to protect the lives of our children above all other concerns. America's infrastructure falls apart? Okay . . . as long as my kids are safe. Custodians are targeted in mass extermination? Alright, as long as my kids and I are safe. Entire swaths of humanity disappeared forever? I am only here to protect my own.

"My son, Graham!" Bentley gasped. "He's an amplifier—he's . . . *the* . . . Amplifier, Phillip. He's . . . he's more powerful than you could know, taking existing powers and extending them by a factor of ten or more. And now *he* has him!"

"Who is *he*?"

"The Superintendent," Bentley replied.

The State Superintendent, as he preferred to be known, had previously been called the Chairman. Before that, he'd been Lionel Milliken. He'd started as a campaign worker for a previous President and parlayed that success into a high party position. Then, he'd helped destroy the party from within, and once it was in chaos, he swooped in to create unity and move the party forward under his own leadership.

Real "cult of personality" stuff.

Soon his true motives came to light, as he first went after the very poorest among us: the homeless, the hungry, those struggling to make rent. And he killed them; he killed them all. Not with policy. Not with new legislation. But with the firepower of the executive order and the national guard. Literal bullets.

Execution task forces. They were officially named the American Beautification Crew, and the ABCs wasted no time following orders, as though many of them had long been hoping for a chance to use their weapons to kill.

Inside of a week he'd wiped out millions of homeless Americans, and he went on the morning shows touting it as a positive thing for the country's image to have our streets be so much cleaner and safer now.

"I guess we thought it would take longer for him to come after custodians," Bentley said, "but after the homeless, those in elder care facilities, and those with disabilities and terminal illnesses, Milliken came after those with superpowers, framing our abilities as genetic defects that would poison the future gene pool for all of humanity. Eugenics as policy."

I'd inadvertently taken my family into hiding just before all custodians needed to go into hiding. Morbidly fortunate timing, I guess.

"And now you need my help," I scoffed. "After all these years, Bent. You screw us all over, disappear, and show up a decade or more later and I'm just supposed to forget all that other stuff?"

"I know it's not easy," he said softly. "I know I'm asking a lot. But I'm telling you the truth, Phillip. You can hook me up to a lie detector or call in an Adjudicator, if there are any left, but I'm not lying."

"Either way, I am guessing my family is no longer safe hiding out here." I was still more angry than anything else.

"I have no idea," Bentley replied. "I found you via an algorithm I developed myself, informed by my many years of history as your friend and battle mate. I doubt the government is anywhere close to finding you."

"But they are looking for me," I added. "Aren't they?"

"They're looking for powers. When a certain type of custodian—usually a physically empowered one, as opposed to a mental like me—uses their powers, an unseen energy field is created, but only temporarily."

"Sounds terrifying."

"Originally they could only tell when custodial powers were used within fifty miles of the Finder. Now that they have my son, that range is greatly increased, probably to as much as five hundred miles."

"They have a machine that can sense when people are using their powers?" I was apoplectic.

"Not a machine, no," he replied gravely. "A man. The Finder is a custodian . . . one with the ability to sense when nearby custodians are using their powers."

"So, they aren't looking for me, at least not here . . . at least not yet. But what if they are looking for you? Or following you?"

"They aren't looking for me. My powers can't even be detected by the Finder!"

"You'll forgive me if I don't take you at your wor—"

"HE HAS MY SON!" Bentley shouted. "What else can I do but seek help from the most powerful person I know?" His words tripped over the choked-down sobs.

I spoke calmly and quietly. "Bent . . . I haven't used my powers since the last time you saw me. I swore it all off. Gave it up. I'm done, man. I have nothing left to give."

"Just because you stopped doesn't mean the tank is empty."

"You don't even—"

"I know *exactly* why you stopped, Phillip. I swear. I even *understand* why you did it. I came here knowing you were a dozen years out of practice. I came here knowing you'd given up being a hero, knowing you hated me. And I did it because I'm exactly *that* desperate. I'm so desperate I'm seeking help from the person I most betrayed. Because . . ." his voice trembled, "I have everything to lose here. I need my boy!"

I heard the unmistakable creak of that nagging front porch floorboard that made noise every time one stepped on it. I immediately looked toward the house to see both my children on the porch, eyes wide at having been caught eavesdropping. I simply stared. A moment later they dashed back inside.

"Great," I spat. "Now I have to explain to them that their mother probably isn't still alive and undo all that shit you just said. Thanks."

"Here," Bentley said, before handing me a small circular device. "You need to find me, just click this button and you'll get my coordinates." I'd used a personal navigator enough to know how it worked, but I guess he was just used to explaining his gadgets to people.

"Thanks," I replied sarcastically. "I look forward to not using it."

"I understand your anger, Phillip," he said, as my door opened for me—I assumed he'd pressed a button to open it. I climbed out, shut the door, and looked back at him through the partially open window. "I just hope you come to realize exactly how dire the situation is for everyone right now," he said, before throwing the car in reverse and backing away.

He's definitely just using my wife to get to me, I thought to myself. *Even if he's not a villain anymore, he's still manipulating me here. Right?*

I watched him back all the way out of our incredibly long dirt driveway before I turned back toward the house. I briefly saw the kids at the screen door before they bolted away to avoid my wrath.

I guess the kids probably thought I had a temper. Or a short fuse.

And maybe I did.

They seemed to fear my anger. I always told myself I was hard on them in order to prepare them for a world that was going to be even harder on them.

Perhaps that's just a line a father tells himself.

Breakfast with teenagers is always quiet. Teenagers require twice the wake-up time that adults and small children do. Often they eat breakfast as a matter of robotic re-creation of past behavior, rather than out of any new impulses.

"So . . ." *Starting out strong,* I thought. "I'm assuming you guys want to talk about last night," I added casually, while dropping scrambled eggs onto Henry's plate.

"HolyCrapWhatYesDadMomPrisonerPowersCrisisAmplifierHolyCow!" They spoke over each other, and I struggled to make sense of what either of them was saying.

I set the pan down and put both palms up in the air at the same time—the family hand-signal for "shut the hell up or you will get grounded." Both kids quieted immediately.

"We're going to go about this in a uniform fashion," I said as I picked up the pan of eggs and continued serving my daughter and then filled my own plate. "Winnie, you're oldest—you go first."

"Aw, man," Henry groaned.

"Shush!" I snapped. And he clammed up.

"Is our mother alive?" Winnie asked.

"No," I replied. "Just because Bentley says he isn't sure doesn't mean your mom is alive. I was there. I saw the explosion. And no one wants her to be alive more than I do," I admitted, my weary sadness obvious.

"But what about his son?" Henry asked.

"Or the Lord Dictator Dude he mentioned," Winnie added.

"I realize we don't get guests very often," I began, "but you both disobeyed here *twice* last night. And I think that needs to be acknowledged first. So . . . eavesdropping . . . good or bad behavior?"

I heard both kids sigh as I walked around the counter.

"Bad," Winnie replied.

"Bad," Henry agreed.

"Well, you know the rules. You have a choice of punishments. You can deep-clean the livestock stalls *or* you can retrace the property boundary of our land . . . on foot, twice."

"Dad, the boundary never changes," Henry said, obviously trying to help me.

"Son, walking and measuring the boundary might just not be solely about the boundary itself." I cocked my head. "I think you need boundary duty today," I smiled.

"Dang it," he cursed.

"Winnie, that puts you on stall-cleaning duty," I declared. "NO USING YOUR POWERS!"

"Why?" she whined.

"If you use your powers you'll finish your punishment in thirty seconds."

"I estimate twenty-eight," she said defiantly.

"Exactly. The punishment isn't just about the task itself, but about the time it takes to complete, during which one might consider making different choices in the future."

"I have to clean all the animal stalls without going fast?"

"Sorry, Winnie," I said, half earnestly. "You're going to have to do it the old-fashioned way."

"Does that mean I can't go fast?" Henry complained.

"You can go as fast as you want, buddy." Even at full speed, Henry was still pretty slow. "But no using your powers either."

Hours later, with both kids asleep, I lay awake in my bunk after tossing and turning for what seemed like a couple of hours, all of it spent wondering how much of what Bentley said I could trust.

Can I even trust any of it at all?

Let's say he's telling the truth . . . he's still asking me to risk my own life and the lives of my kids to help him save his son. What nerve!

But if he is telling the truth, then it's a lot more than just his son that's at stake. If he's right, the entire Earth could be decimated by this insane man running the country right now.

Is there a way I can help without actually using my powers? No. No, of course not. I can't leave my children here alone, so if I go . . . they go. And once my kids are present . . . how do I focus on anything except keeping them safe? I guess I could ask Patrick to watch them, but that could end up doing more harm than having them tag along with me.

No, the best thing is to stay put. Keep with the plan. Stay obscure, in hiding, drawing no attention to ourselves.

4

THE PEARS

We'd gone into town one more time, only to find Zip's General Store's lights out for good. The entire block—that's how small the town was—was dark and abandoned.

I guess I'm not sure what I had expected, though it was good to get the kids out of the house anytime I could.

We stopped by the Willister Orchards on the way back. No one seemed to be around, but the pears were plentiful. We picked a bunch and left some cash in the mailbox before we made our way back home.

Pear this. Pear that. The kids had grand recipe ideas for using the pears, most of which required a lot more work than either child was currently prepared for.

I had other ideas.

Talking with Bentley had left me reflecting on one thing: that, no matter my intentions, no matter even if I had done the right thing, my decisions had robbed my kids of a lot of normal-kid stuff. School dances, street fairs and carnivals, trick-or-treating.

Perhaps worse than merely depriving them of the fun stuff was the fact that they didn't even know it. They had no idea what a normal kid's life was like. We were so far removed from society they didn't have any idea what they were missing out on.

And that made me sad. Seems like my entire life I've been making hard decisions for what felt like good reasons that ended up with unforeseen consequences.

Maybe everyone feels like that. But it seemed I'd spent so much time on regret that, at some point, I started letting it make decisions for me.

We weren't going to leave our secluded little farm or anything drastic—especially now that custodians were being actively hunted. I wasn't going to start letting them have sleepovers or visit the zoo. But gosh darn it, we were gonna have some fun.

"Pear pie!" Winnie shouted, running from the car to the house.

"Pear fritters!" Hen called after her.

I trudged slowly behind them, giant bag of pears in my arm, smiling. "We're not going to cook 'em," I said just as they reached the porch. "Well, not at first at least."

I bypassed the porch and continued around the side of the house, setting the bag of pears down next to a tree while I continued out to the shed.

Back in the corner I found a few old feed troughs no longer in use and dragged one out of the shed and back toward the house.

The kids' curiosity finally got the best of them as they rounded the corner of the house.

"Dad, what are you doing?"

I dropped the trough directly under the garden hose spigot, turned to Winnie, and smiled. "We're going to play a game, Winnie."

I turned the spigot on and water poured into the trough. I just stood there, arms folded, looking and feeling very proud of myself.

Henry kept looking between the trough and me, occasionally glancing at his sister. It was clear he was trying to work it out. "This game seems more like chores," he said, confused.

I just laughed a little. "You guys stay here." I walked around and went inside the house. I grabbed some towels from the closet and went back outside.

"Dad, is this another one of your weird life lessons like how you taught us to swim?"

"Or that time you let us eat poisonous berries so we would develop respect for nature's plants?"

"Those berries were largely harmless and a tummy ache is a better lesson than just my saying 'Don't eat those.' And no, this is not a life lesson. I told you. It's a game. My dad taught me and my brother this game when we were little." I tossed the towels onto the ground and inspected the level of water in the trough. "I think we're just about ready to go here."

I leaned over and turned the water off. I was giddy with excitement. I bent down, grabbed the bag of pears, and dumped them all into the trough to the collective gasp of my two children.

"Okay, who wants to go first?"

They were stone silent.

"Who wants to go first?" I repeated.

Winnie finally spoke up cautiously, "Are we supposed to count them?"

"Count them? Goodness no! You're supposed to bob for them!" I grinned ear to ear like I'd just told a joke to them and was awaiting praise or applause.

They continued to be confused.

"Bobbing for apples, only this time it's pears! That's the game!"

"So do we use a fishing rod?" Henry asked.

I knew they'd never played it, but I hadn't expected their utter bafflement at the concept. "No, you use your face! You put your hands behind your back and you can only use your face to get the apples—I mean pears. You have to find one with your face and then bite it to pull it out!"

"And then what?"

"You eat it!"

"Do you keep score? Person with the most fruits wins?"

"No, you just . . . you're just trying to get your own pear, just the one pear."

"How is this a game, Dad?" Winnie was growing a little frustrated. "It sounds like you just want me to dunk my head underwater before eating a pear. How does that equate to fun?"

"It's not as easy as you might think," I teased.

"It actually doesn't sound easy at all—to be honest, it sounds difficult."

"It is difficult!" I exclaimed happily.

Henry chimed in. "Wouldn't it just be easier to eat the pear without bothering to dunk yourself in a trough first?"

"Well, yes, son," I countered, "if eating the pear were the only concern. It's easier to just buy pigeon from the Harrisons down the river than it is to shoot, skin, and prepare your own . . . but meat you put the work in for always tastes better, right?"

"Henry doesn't like pigeon," Winnie reminded me, a little coldly.

"Right, okay, but the point still stands, okay? Henry, you like fish, right? The trout you catch tastes better than the one you bring home from the store, doesn't it?"

"I don't think we ever had any store-bought trout," he stated flatly.

I sighed. "Well, how about you guys watch me go. It can be pretty funny to watch someone flail around in the tank trying to grab a pear!" I kneeled down in front of the trough. "I'll tell you what, if you guys don't think it's funny watching me bob for pears, then you don't have to do it."

They accepted my proposal the way teenagers do, by staring blankly at me and saying nothing.

I had fond memories of this game, though none of them were visual. One of the things I loved as a kid about bobbing for apples—or whatever floating fruit—was that everyone was basically blind when doing it—there wasn't the usual built-in disadvantage for me to participate.

With a cackle of delight, I clasped my hands behind my back and dove my head down into the water.

It was colder than I expected. The whole family had been known to grab a long drink of water from this spigot, and the water was always cool to the touch and a pleasant temperature to drink, but never seemed particularly cold. This water was cold. I spent the first five seconds just shaking off the shock.

I felt something bounce by my nose and gnawed toward it briefly, but missed. Honestly there were pears everywhere. I'd put too many in. And yet the trough was large enough they were all moving around in the churning water.

Probably should have cleaned the trough before doing this.

Another pear bumped my chin, and I pulled away, up, and then bit down . . . but I missed slightly and the pear glanced off my teeth.

I came up for a loud, gasping breath and immediately dunked myself again, determined to somehow both show the kids how hard this was but also get it over with so it could be their turn.

I tried a new strategy I called the Hover.

I placed my face just above the water, the tip of my nose just touching the surface, and I waited for an unassuming pear to wander into my trap. The benefit of the hover method is that it allowed me to continue breathing until my prey was at hand, rather than holding my breath while completely submerged.

I heard the kids' feet scurry around so they could get a better look at what I was doing.

After about ten seconds, a fat pear drifted into my bite zone, just barely nudging my nose as it came through. I opened my jaw as wide as it would go, tip of my nose still in the water, and when the moment was right . . . I snapped my jaw closed.

I jerked my head up out of the trough and laughed hysterically as I shook my head from side to side to get rid of excess water before bringing my hand up to my face, grabbing the pear, and taking a victorious bite!

I chewed loudly while toweling off my face and my head. "Alright," I said, "who wants to go—"

I removed the towel mid-syllable to find myself alone. No kids around. No one. They'd taken me at my word, and had gone inside the moment they felt this entire exercise was unfun.

Only Monster remained, head cocked at the absurdity of my behavior.

"Good boy," I said, petting him. "Good boy." I sat down on the ground and lay back on the wet grass and sighed heavily.

My kids hate me.

A few hours later, as bedtime loomed and after at least five different pear dishes had been created by my young chef children, I began my usual nightly checklist.

"Alright, guys," I said loudly as they continued cleaning up the kitchen. "Chickens!"

"Fed," Henry replied.

"Check. Horses?"

Winnie this time. "Walked, brushed, stalls cleaned, fed."

"Check," I replied. "Pig and cattle!"

Winnie again: "Pastured, fed, safely in the barn."

"Check. Garden?"

Henry's turn to respond: "Harvested, pruned, fertilized, watered."

I heard a dish break as it hit the floor, a casualty of my insistence on combining chores with learning. I ignored it. "Check. Fish basket?"

"Oh crap," Henry breathed before he could stop himself. "I mean shoot! I may have forgotten to check the fish basket today, sir," he said, panicky.

We had a large fish basket in the nearby stream. We had all kinds of fish in there, but mostly seemed to catch perch, walleye, whitefish, and trout. We averaged about four fish a day, though we threw back the ones that were too small to get much meat off of. If we went out even further to the river, we'd catch even more variety. But a fish basket is a way to catch fish with very little effort.

Well, I should say very little effort once the basket itself is built. It's a basic animal trap concept that has been around for centuries, with a large-mouth opening that narrows greatly as the fish enter the trap . . . then the way out is unclear and super narrow even if it's found, and the fish end up trapped.

"Alright," I answered. "Well, you're going to need to go out there and check that basket before you go to bed." I was a stickler for chores. I told myself I was teaching the kids discipline, but part of me always wondered if maybe I was just anal retentive about keeping a schedule.

Henry's shoulders sagged, even as he continued drying a plate with a dish towel. "Can't I just go in the morning?" This was a common tactic both kids used, though it had never once been successful.

"What's the point of giving you responsibilities if you only want to put them off?"

"I never asked for you to give me any responsibilities," he barked.

"Dad," Winnie interrupted before things could escalate, "why don't you let me go?"

I took a deep breath and let it out slowly—the unofficial signal that she could continue making her argument.

"I can get there and back in about five seconds, give or take a second. Then it's done; it's over. And Henry can pay me back by tending to the horses tomorrow."

One parenting technique of which I was proud was having encouraged thoughtful debate, provided one came armed with logic, and an alternate solution. So it was hard for me to find fault with Winnie's plan. And I did, on some level, appreciate her stepping in to take care of her little brother.

"Approved," I finally breathed, just to feel a small gust of wind as she ran by and out the front door.

"Your sister really loves you," I said to Henry in the silence.

"I know." Sounded like he meant it.

"Don't think I won't check up on you about those horses tomorrow," I added.

"Yes, sir."

And that's when Winnie breezed back in, stopping in the kitchen. "Two large trout and a medium walleye," she declared.

"Alright, we've got some trout in the fridge from yesterday; let's add them to that stash and fry up some fish tomorrow night."

"Alright!" Winnie cheered.

"Awesome," Henry added.

I wouldn't say we had a healthy diet here, but it was rare that we fried anything, so it could have been root vegetables from the garden and the kids would have been happy to fry it up in a pan with some light breading.

"Okay, kitchen looks clean, chores are all finished . . . why don't you guys head to bed."

They hurried by, each taking a moment to hug me, before scampering up the ladder to the half-second story.

The two kids shared what amounted to a loft, with a single wall between them. I slept downstairs, just off the kitchen, in a mostly-closed room that had no door.

That night I struggled to fall asleep. I was imagining my kids as young adults, where I could no longer protect them and keep them from harm . . . and what the world might look like when that happened . . . and it left me tossing and turning until the wee hours of the morning.

5

THE ASSAULT

The perimeter alarm went off around 2:00 a.m.

Both kids were down the ladder quickly and met me in the living room of the cottage.

"Did you walk that perimeter two nights ago like I told you to?" I whispered.

"Yes, sir," Henry whispered back emphatically. "Everything was green."

"Green" was our family's word for "A-OK" or "good to go," as in a green light. I'm really not sure why so much of my parenting style held elements of military verbiage. I'd never served in the military. Maybe I just saw my role sometimes as more of a drill instructor than as a comforter. That couldn't be a good thing, but I didn't have time to wonder about it now.

"Okay, so then we have to assume the perimeter has been breached. Do you guys remember the protocol?"

"Dog, doors, basement," they said in unison. I didn't have time to be as proud as I wanted to be.

"Alright," I said. "Henry, call the dog. Winnie, open the floor door."

Because I was a paranoid off-the-grid type of father, I had a bail-out shelter under the cottage that we all called "the basement." It had enough food to last for at least a year, along with a small supply of books, magazines, and a few games. It wasn't a fallout shelter, and it wouldn't protect us from radiation or even a nearby explosion . . . but it just might hide us.

I didn't have time to wonder how they'd found us, though it would be obvious later on when I finally put my mind to it. I didn't have time to wonder how many there were or what their payload or armament was.

I just knew someone or something had crossed our perimeter line and I was in fight-or-flight mode to protect my children.

It wasn't a grizzly bear or a cougar. These were highly calibrated machines, capable of telling animals apart from human beings—though it would also have sounded a different alarm if a bear or a mountain lion wandered through, because we weren't really looking for company of the military *or* the grizzly variety.

Once we were all in the basement, including Monster, I hit the kill switch. This cut all power to the house and forced the enemy to switch to night vision or thermal vision.

The basement was crude and small, but I'd been smart in designing it, and had lined it with space blankets—you can get these at survival camping shops or even army/navy surplus stores sometimes. They block thermal and night vision. I doubted these soldiers had infrared vision as well, but the space blankets would even protect us from that.

They could burn the cabin down, and we'd die. Or they could find the microscopic seams in the flooring that hid the door to the basement, and we'd get arrested and later probably die. Otherwise, we should be safe from detection, as long as we remained quiet.

Of course, I'd installed cameras all around the house when we'd first moved in, but the video feed access was hardwired into my office—I didn't want to send it over the air and risk someone possibly intercepting it.

I had no way to know who tripped the perimeter sensor or how many were with them, but I could now hear at least two different helicopters overhead. There had to be a lot of them out there. Fear rushed in like a deep breath of rancid air.

I gasped and went down to one knee, as an anxiety attack approached. This is what Bentley warned about, the police state gobbling up all custodians.

"Dad, are you okay?" Winnie asked.

I put my finger to my lips emphatically and then pointed above.

She nodded, then zipped to my side in a nanosecond and whispered, "What's wrong, Daddy?"

But it was too late. Panic had already gripped me.

I can't believe this is happening. I gave up being a hero to avoid these attacks and now it's happening again anyway!

Upstairs and outside, the soldiers drew nearer and nearer to the cottage. I assumed they'd already cleared the barns and the chicken coop. I hoped they didn't step on any eggs.

Sensing the panic building only made me panic more. It had been years since I'd experienced one of these, but suddenly everything came rushing back.

Winnie saw me wheezing and gasping for breath, and somehow found and brought me a small paper bag, which I loosely remembered being the dominoes container on our game shelf. I put the bag to my mouth and breathed deliberately.

Slowly but surely, I regained my rhythm, even as the cabin doors could be heard being rammed open. A swarm of footsteps entered and pounded like thunder above us.

"Clear!" I heard someone yell, followed by three more shouts of "Clear!"

But by then the soldiers upstairs were nearly upon us.

I gathered the kids and the dog in one of the corners of the small make-shift basement, kneeled, and began a whispered speech.

"I love you all. You know that long ago I swore off using my powers ever again. And I had really, really good reasons. My powers have mostly only led to death and destruction, and that kind of thing takes a toll on a person." I paused, the sound of the soldiers closer and closer.

"I'm not evil. I'm not an idiot. My vow doesn't supersede my love for you. I *will* use my powers here and now to protect you. Just, please don't think less of me afterward, I beg of you."

Both kids nodded, seemingly in awe of the moment and also my state-ment. The dog just leaned in and licked my face.

I went down on both knees, bowed my head, and crossed my arms in front of my chest in an *X* formation. And then I asked for power.

You see, my ability has always relied on the cooperation of the atoms around me and the atoms around the objects I want to move.

We are all just a collection of atoms, of course. Human skin, no matter what your perception is, is *not* a solid substance. It's a collection of atoms . . . they just so happen to be so tightly bound that they end up forming what *seems* like a solid substance—aka skin.

And all the matter around us on Earth—and likely all the matter in the universe—is also made up of the same atoms.

My power is the ability to reshape those atoms. Now, maybe I have authority over the atoms and could do my own bidding without a second thought, but I always subconsciously ask permission.

With the incoming forces, I was not surprised to feel the power flowing to me rapidly. The atoms all around me were willing to bend to my will, should I ask them to.

The noise above raged as the soldiers tossed the house for any evidence of our presence or any clue that could lead them to us.

It's only a matter of time before they find us, I told myself.

I resigned myself to giving in to the Animal.

Over these last couple decades, I'd taken to calling my power the An-imal—actually that's not true . . . it wasn't the power itself . . . it was the personal impact from *using* the power that had haunted me for twenty-plus years.

Like Bruce Banner and the Hulk, the Animal was not something I felt I could fully control, especially not after nearly twenty years of dormancy. It wanted out. It screamed for release.

And I knew it was only a matter of seconds before I gave in. Not just be-cause the Animal's call was strong, but also because my own desire to protect my children was strong. If these soldiers above got close . . . there was no telling the carnage I might rain down upon them once I let it all loose.

Imagine owning the fastest car in the world, and you put it in a garage for twenty years. Then you take it out to race again. Now imagine if that car was sentient. How much pent-up "ready to race" angst must be in there . . . that was me. Years of my little legs churning like a Flinstones car while being held in place by the fingers of God . . . only now I was finally about to be let go.

I looked at my kids, only to find two absolutely terrified faces.

Oh no! I actually have to parent right now in this moment?!

"It's going to be fine," I assured them, knowing it actually probably would be fine for now. I would obliterate every being assaulting our home and we would live to see tomorrow. But then what?

I didn't have the luxury of considering the step beyond this next one, only this next one, which would keep my family safe in the short term.

"I love you," I said quietly, as I bent down and prepared to blast everything within one hundred yards far, far away from my current position.

Ooph!

I knew that sound. Not just the type of sound; I knew that sound specifically.

Before I could speak or even think, I felt a hand being placed upon my back before another sudden—

Ooph!

Emmaline! She's alive?! My wife is . . . alive?!

Suddenly we were standing on a remote, lonely stretch of road.

"I had that situation under control!" I barked instinctively.

"Right. That's why you were panicking."

"I didn't need your help!"

"You haven't used your powers in a generation, of course you needed help."

"I can't believe you're going to play savior here after all these years."

"And I can't believe you're gonna play victim here after all these years."

Both she and I panted as we gained back our breath. Soon the deep breathing turned to smiles, and then laughter. Without a word we embraced as hard as any two humans ever embraced.

Then we kissed.

"Kids," I smiled, "meet your mother."

6

THE ROAD

"I thought you were dead!" I laughed as I spoke, so full was my heart with joy. I kissed her face all over in between statements. "I saw you die!"

"Obviously not," she countered.

"How? What even happened?"

"Not now," she clarified before turning to our kids. "My God. You're so big. You're so beautiful. I missed you both so much." She knelt and hugged them.

Both kids looked at me in confusion. Winnifred had been pretty young when Emmaline died—disappeared—and Henry even younger. They had few memories of her other than the stories I had told them.

I smiled warmly at them both, hoping to convey that things were okay and they were safe. It had to be a weird feeling, though, to live in the woods your whole life with a strict father and then suddenly meet your mother directly after your first experience teleporting.

"Okay," she said, matter-of-factly. "Again, more time to get to know each other later. First things first—Phillip, what the hell is going on?"

"You're asking me?! I was just about to ask you!"

"All I know is I got a proximity alarm notice and showed up just in time to save your asses," she explained, without humor.

"How did you have access to our proximity bea—. . . Bentley," I breathed, answering my own question. "Bentley put a tracker on my land, didn't he? He didn't just *think* you had survived the attack I'd witnessed, he already knew it! You contacted Bentley before you contacted me?!" I was speaking as my brain reached each new conclusion, with no real filter in the moment.

"I had to make sure you weren't already being watched! I had to make sure it was safe, which it ultimately was not!" She made a bit of sense.

"No one ever caught a whiff of us before last night. Bentley's the one who was being watched and he brought this on all of us!"

"Enough!" Winnie yelled, somewhat surprisingly.

We both turned to look at her.

"We are standing in the middle of a highway!"

I turned to my wife. "Why did you teleport us to a highway?"

"Because no one uses them anymore and I was just trying to get us away from your cabin where, I will note, you were about to hurt and kill some people before I showed up, so you're welcome."

I sighed. "How far are we from the cabin?" I asked.

"What does that matter?" she countered, still wanting to fight.

"Because they can now track when powers are used by custodians to a five-hundred-mile range, and they were already closing on my cabin with full forces, so they will definitely figure out where we are right now if you only jumped us inside a five-hundred-mile radius. So where the hell are we?"

"Inside that radius, I'm afraid." It was Bentley, walking onto the highway from the gas station to the west.

"You knew about the five hundred miles thing and you didn't tell her?" I was processing so much new information it was inevitable I was going to get exasperated.

"We were communicating by blind drop," he explained as he drew closer. "There's a natural delay. I didn't have time to tell her."

"Can we just get off the road!" Winnie yelled.

And she was right.

She didn't have any idea how few people were out traveling America by highways right now, but she was definitely correct that we were more findable here than any non-middle-of-the-road place.

"She's right," I said.

"Everyone in," Emmaline replied, putting her hand out face down.

"Are we sure we should teleport? If we're inside the radius, then they can see us use our powers again, right?"

"But if we jump to outside the radius," Bentley added, "they'll have no clue where we went. We could end up in China and they wouldn't know. Actually, we need to be at least five hundred miles from the original cabin *and* at least five hundred miles from this location." He looked to Em. "Understood?"

"Yep," she replied.

"Okay. Everyone in," I declared. "Let's get out of here and then figure out how to stay alive."

Everyone's hands came into the center, piling on top of each other, until the last hand hit.

Ooph!

"Okay, now where are we?" I bellowed.

"Uh," Emmaline said slowly, "somewhere fifty miles or so northeast of Las Vegas." There was a pause and then, "It's pretty cold here at night."

"Why did you bring us here?" I asked.

"I panicked," she replied. "I just did the math and took off toward the first place I knew for sure met the criteria."

"Well," Bentley offered, "they definitely won't be looking for us here."

"Alright," I conceded for now. "But let's at least find a place to stay that has heat." I blinked twice to change my vision to thermal. Within minutes we found the nearest town and were all checked into a tiny motel and hunkered down for the night.

Emmaline and I shared a room with our kids, which made it difficult to continue our very necessary conversation about how the hell she was still alive and what both of us had been through in the last ten years.

There were two queen beds, and each of us occupied one of them along with a sleeping child.

I was surprised when she used sign language, even though we'd both learned it long ago.

Delilah Darlington, who had been in that Special Education class with me my first year of custodian high school, had also gone to Goodspeed University with Em and I. Somewhere around our junior year she came back into our regular social circle when she shared a history class with Emmaline. We were fast friends for years, first with Delilah and then also with her husband, Jeff.

Sign language became natural to both of us as those friendships grew, and when our kids were born, we found signing to be a convenient way of communicating without the toddlers knowing what we were saying.

It was after Jeff and Delilah were killed by the government's anti-custodian goon squad that I'd had enough and moved the kids way off the grid.

"I've missed you so much," Em signed.

"Me as well," I signed back, feeling rusty immediately. *"How did you survive that boom and how did you live beyond that?"* Again, my signing wasn't perfect, but I hoped she knew what I was asking.

"You guys doing all the sign language is not making me feel super confident," Henry said aloud.

Both Emmaline and I immediately shushed him.

"He only pretended to kill me. I've been forced into his service ever since, until I broke free two weeks ago via intelligence I thought had come from Bentley," she assured me.

"He screwed everyone over last time," I began, before she cut me off.

"I don't get that sense this time, Phillip, I really don't. I think he's here to help."

"Only because his kid has been kidnapped."

"Stop being so cynical. You're a hero, for Pete's sake! Go, save a life!"

As usual, she won.

"Fine!" I yelled out loud, before signing, *"this conversation isn't over."*

"Whatever helps you sleep at night," she signed back, before adding that she loved me and hoped I would sleep well.

We awoke hot, each of us drenched in sweat.

Southern Nevada mornings were as hot as their nights were cold, it appeared. No trouble—we had a shower, and even though the hot water gave out after Em and Winnie were done, Henry and I were perfectly willing to shower in freezing cold water because of how sweaty we were.

Vegas itself was mostly dark, to hear our hosts tell it. Towns with electricity were few and far between.

There were many factors to how and why North America cleared out so fast. A lot of it had to do with the Superintendent's scorched-earth attack on custodians. There was audio of him at a fundraiser saying, "I don't care if I kill ten innocent humans in the act of killing one custodian; that's how dangerous these superpowered beings are!" Of course, he denied saying it and said the clip was fake. And his supporters didn't even seem bothered by the clip at all, parroting the line during marches and protest rallies.

But there was also the flu surge to blame, as well as mass migrations away from North America to more welcoming countries like New Zealand, Brazil, and France.

Then there was the very natural human-on-human crime that is likely to occur in times of famine, blackout, or mass destruction . . . looting, lying, stealing, killing . . . self-preservation over rule of law. That only brought out more oversight from the government in the form of drones.

At any given moment in America you might've been on camera due to government drones. If those drones suspected you of being a custodian, then the kill squads showed up pretty quickly.

We knew that the drones couldn't tell from the air if someone was a custodian or not. But the Department of Homeland Security—or DHS— officials were still stopping an awful lot of regular humans to interrogate. Having powers didn't matter anymore, in terms of whether or not the government was willing to use, abuse, incarcerate, or kill you in the name of stamping out custodians.

So most places resembled ghost towns, because everyone was hiding. Or gone. Or dead.

There were rumors that a lot of Vegas citizens had gone down into the city's infamous aqueduct tunnels where homeless and nomadic folks have thrived for decades.

There were rumors some had gone up into the mountains, where structures were rare and the terrain less likely to draw the interest of the drones.

Basically, we needed to be more than careful. And if we wanted to travel across America, we would need a lot of planning, a lot of help, and a lot of luck.

And unfortunately, we needed to travel across America if we were to rescue Bentley's son, who we believed was being held captive in Washington, DC, where the Superintendent was based.

The Superintendent's endgame—regardless of how many custodians he captured in the meantime—was to blow up the moon. Yeah, I know . . . it was extreme. He'd given several public speeches about how the moon was the basis of the custodians' powers.

Several prominent scientists and most major world leaders denounced this belief as dangerous and unfounded by science. But this did little to stop the Superintendent's plan. He aimed to combine two of his captive heroes—a Fireballer and an Amplifier—to take the moon out in a huge explosion.

This was a terrifying thought.

But he couldn't do it without the use of Bentley's kid, the Amplifier. So if we could get to the kid and rescue him before the moon plan was enacted, we could stop a catastrophe.

Maybe.

7

STEALTH

So how do we go from southern Nevada to Washington, DC, without getting noticed by the power-detector guy or any of the drones or any of the satellites they might've been controlling up above?

We all threw out ideas, but ultimately the most basic concept turned out to be the best: combine all of the ideas.

The plan was to mix up our travel mode as often as every day or so, driving one day, walking another, traveling via waterways. We also decided to create a path to DC that was . . . less than direct.

Bentley drew up a route that zigged and zagged unnaturally, but it would get us to our destination while simultaneously making it harder for us to be tracked or followed. If we were captured on foot by a satellite headed in one direction . . . well, the next day we would be in a boat going a different direction.

Bentley, true to form, also had a few new gadgets and gizmos that would be helpful on our journey. The most important one was a satellite tracker. He balked at that name, because the tracking of the satellites' trajectories had already been done on his computer. The watch he gave me, which I called the satellite tracker, was merely a modified timepiece that let me know when any of the government-controlled surveillance satellites were about to fly overhead.

There were dozens of these satellites, of course, but they were moving so quickly that none would be above our position for more than a few minutes at a time. Assuming Bentley had correctly identified and logged all the surveillance birds, we would be able to take cover and make ourselves scarce every time one went by overhead, thereby eliminating one of the enemy's means of tracking or following us.

The first leg would be a drive from our near-Vegas location northeast to Denver. From there we intended to move east and up into Nebraska, where we'd catch the Platte River.

We'd ride the Platte River down to the Missouri River, and then ride that into St. Louis to meet up with the mighty Mississippi. But we'd hop off the Mississippi pretty quick once we got to Memphis.

At some point in Tennessee, we would be making use of the now-defunct railroad system—one of the ways the Superintendent hoped to flush out custodians was by cutting supply lines to all major cities and towns, from the trucking industry to the railroad industry to the shipping industry. He just . . . shut it all down. No one was getting anything delivered from half a country away ever again.

The railroad tracks would make an excellent path for us to travel, probably on a modified vehicle, and would certainly be something the satellites and drones were ignoring altogether.

There were more legs and turns after Tennessee, but we all agreed we needed to keep the plan fluid; we had no clue what we might face in this journey, and the best plan always has a few backup options. There were plenty of rivers, roads, and train tracks between here and DC. We would follow the plan until a new plan was required by circumstances.

We needed a vehicle, of course, and our hosts, the owners of the motel, were happy to ferry us back to Vegas. They seemed to know we were in hiding, whether or not they knew we were custodians.

In Vegas there were all sorts of abandoned vehicles for us to steal. Bentley said it wasn't stealing since we were in an apocalypse-type situation, but I still felt a little bad about it.

Tractor trailers were largely extinct on the roads today, since the union had been shut down and the orders stopped coming in. But there were still semis on the highways—they were just government semis these days, typically painted with an American flag motif on the cab and an all-navy-blue trailer.

We briefly considered finding an abandoned truck and painting it to match the government's color scheme, but Bentley worried each official truck had a tracker beacon, and our fake truck would stand out like a sore thumb by not having its own.

And while interstate travel was largely diminished, and the government was cracking down on shipping, there were still trucks on the road. Smaller trucks. Milk trucks, meat trucks, fruit and produce trucks. The Superintendent had gone out of his way to tell Americans that he didn't want them to starve or die . . . he just wanted them to start relying on their local communities.

America had far too long done far too much, he argued, to shoulder the burden of lazy communities. By forcing them all to come together and work together—by killing the shipping industry—he argued he was helping them form bonds of neighborly friendship.

Of course, by forcing small communities around the country to look inward for supplies and food, he was subtly encouraging distrust of other neighboring communities. And he was making it easier to control the narrative of the news cycle by preventing external discussion.

Best of all, he was creating towns and cities that were absolutely primed to narc on any newcomer or strange visitor as a possible custodian. He was creating communities immune to empathy.

Regardless of all that . . . he still allowed local deliveries within two hundred miles—his "community boundary range." And that meant we could drive a small refrigerated truck from Vegas to Denver without raising any suspicion at all.

Bentley did a quick search in his database for refrigerated food companies in the area, and in no time at all we were pulling a bunch of garbage out of the back of a truck to make room for the people.

"Are we there yet?" Henry asked.

Emmaline and Winnie both turned to him with an identical look of shock and disdain—seeing them react in sync was a sudden, not-subtle reminder they had a lot of the same DNA.

Henry didn't even need to be verbally shushed to realize he should shut up, and he went back to gazing out the window.

"How do we know, once we get to DC, how to find your son?" I asked, quite casually. I was driving the vehicle currently, but Bentley was in the passenger seat, and I was mostly just trying to make conversation to pass the time.

"He has a homing beacon on him," Bentley stated.

I drove a few moments before responding. "Does he know he has a beacon on him?" Let's just call it a hunch as to why I asked.

Bentley's initial silence spoke volumes.

"He doesn't!" I said, mostly laughing. "Poor kid's been walking around in middle school thinking he's his own person, but in reality his every move is being examined."

"It's not like that," Bentley objected. "His power is so unique . . . so rare . . . we just couldn't risk the chance that he might be kidnapped, which is exactly what ended up happening, I might add." Bentley had yet to tell me what had become of his wife, Penelope. The omission was glaring enough I was afraid to ask about it.

I hadn't even thought that far ahead. I was just making a joke. "Yeah . . . sorry," I said quietly. "Didn't really think it through."

"It's fine," he replied. "No one who doesn't have an Amplifier kid would give it as much thought as I have."

"And he can really do this?" I asked cautiously. "He can really amplify powers as much as ten times?"

Bentley sighed in a very concerned manner. "He could probably go even higher if they pushed him. He's a sweetheart of a kid, I swear, but he's sitting on more raw power inside him than I've ever seen in any single custodian. I'm really worried."

For Bentley to say this was quite a statement. To date, it was a commonly held belief amongst custodians that I myself, Phillip Sallinger, was the most powerful custodian on Earth, despite my long absence from any meaningful hero work or power usage.

Bentley's kid must be one powerful little sucker.

And that made sense, if he was an Amplifier; he'd be able to take my most-powerful moment and magnify it to unthinkable reaches.

I shuddered. "That's terrifying." I paused, still processing. "I really hope we get to your kid before he becomes part of some awful event. That would leave lasting impressions."

"It would, but if I'm honest, I just want my son back. I miss him," Bentley said, flashing a rare moment of emotional rawness.

"Then let's go get him."

"Are we there yet?" Henry asked yet again.

"I'm considering using my powers for the first time in eighteen years just to muzzle your incessantly complaining ass," I barked at my own flesh-and-blood son.

He quieted immediately.

"I'm sorry," I offered quickly. "Tempers are short now, and that's no excuse, and I'm sorry I snapped at you." I meant it. "But you have *got* to stop asking if we're there yet because its repetition is driving everyone except you absolutely insane." I meant that too.

We were nearing Denver, and my infrared vision was picking up plenty of heat up ahead, indicating there was still a large group of people there who still had electricity.

"Do you want me to take over driving?" Emmaline was riding shotgun now.

"No, I'm fine," I lied.

"You look pretty tired."

"You look beautiful."

"Don't change the subject," she scolded.

"I'm not. Your being beautiful is a universal constant. Whenever I bring it up, I'm not changing the subject, I'm just breathing. You are air, and I have been the clouds in your way for far too long."

She blushed a bit. "Since when did you get so poetic?"

"Since my dead wife came back to life," I smiled. I think, if we had been alone, we would have chosen this moment to pull over for a bit of quality time. But since we were *not* alone, I kept driving and she tried quickly to change the subject.

"I'm serious about driving," she clarified. "You don't have to do all this alone."

"I'm not trying to do all this alone. In fact, I very much do not want to do any of this. I was quite fine living off the grid with my children—our children—thank you very much."

There was a long pause before she spoke again. "I'm so sorry, Phillip."

"Sorry? For what?"

"You thought I was gone forever and it caused you to make some . . . extreme life decisions. Decisions I am sure you felt you had to make to protect your family. I'm sorry you had to go through that."

"Yeah, well, it's in the past. Nothing we can do about it now. Besides, I never blamed you; I blamed the Superintendent. Because he's the one to blame. He's the one that killed Delilah and Jeff and hundreds of other custodians and millions of innocent Americans."

We were rounding a huge curve in the interstate, and even as I spoke to Emmaline my brain took time to appreciate the gorgeous scenery of the landscape around me. Sight was new enough to me that I still regularly took time to appreciate it.

"Even if I'm not to blame I can still feel sorry for you."

"I get it. I appreciate it. I just don't want to talk about it right now."

"Mister Therapy doesn't want to talk about it?" Her tone was playful, but I wasn't in a place to receive it correctly.

"Mister Therapy? Mister Therapy?!" I had long since raised my voice before I realized it, even though I was still being playful in my tone.

If Bentley or either of the kids in the back had been asleep, they were now awake.

"Sounds like you guys had a great marriage," Henry snarked.

"Shut up," we sniped at him in unison.

A brief lull was followed by Emmaline piping back up. "I do have a question, though, about the whole off-the-grid situation."

"Oh no," I breathed.

"Is . . . that a sensitive subject? 'Oh no, someone asked about our cabin'? 'Oh no, someone found out we grew our own vegetables'?"

"'Oh no, there's a police roadblock up ahead,'" I blurted out.

"Aw, crap," she sighed.

8

DETOURS

"Shit!" I shouted, unable to censor myself in time.

I felt the scolding gaze of nearly everyone except Bentley, who had heard me say much worse.

"We have about three miles," I guessed, "before this vehicle will arrive at a police checkpoint. All ideas are welcome; good ideas go to the front of the line."

"I can teleport most of us away from here," Emmaline said quickly.

"Alright," I allowed. "But how do we know there aren't drones or satellites in this area that would catch your use of powers and bring even more heat to this area?"

Bentley handled the reply. "Would they have a roadblock in an area they already had covered by satellite or drone? I don't think so. In fact, in the modern world, a roadblock is the *least* efficient way to catch a fugitive."

"Okay," I said. "But we need someone left behind to drive this thing that can get through a police checkpoint. That's not Bentley . . . they tracked him to our house. It's not Emmaline . . . she's an escaped convict in their eyes. It's not me, because I'm still stupidly famous for things I haven't done in nearly twenty years . . . which leaves two . . . only one of which is close to legal driving age . . ."

We all turned toward Winnie and Henry, but mostly Winnie.

"I've only had two driving lessons!" she implored.

But the decision was already made.

"Is it ready?" I panicked.

"I said give me a minute!" Bentley barked back.

"We do not have a minute!"

"Give me whatever we have then! And shut the hell up while I work!"

Winnifred didn't have a driver's license. She'd been taught to drive the family truck by me, but she wasn't legal on the road, per se. So in the 2.2 miles remaining, Bentley was racing to make a fake ID that would fool the state troopers up ahead.

"I can't believe I'm breaking the law to create a fake ID so that we can continue breaking the law," Bentley breathed.

"You can't?" I asked, shocked. "The guy who sucked up most of Earth's energy to find and kill his own father is gonna lecture us about illegal use of powers?" I was ready to fight, but I also knew my tone alone would shut Bentley down.

"You're right," he said meekly. "You're right."

No one said anything for several moments until Em got impatient. "How long until we're done here?"

"Just about thirty seconds," Henry replied—he was holding the stopwatch.

"You are really pushing it!" I yelled.

"I didn't set the parameters, Phillip."

The roadblock grew closer and closer.

"Anytime now," I begged. "Remember, Winnie, you are a new hire bringing an empty truck to Denver to pick up your first load to deliver to Vegas, okay?"

"Annnnd, done," he finally announced. "Winnie, here's your fake ID." There was a slight pause as she accepted the ID. "Everyone else, get in here and let's get out of here. Winnie, don't forget to hit the brakes!"

Hands went into the center, and next thing I knew we were on a rocky hilltop with a strong wind at our backs.

"If you ever leave me alone like that again I will disown you, change my name, run away, and die homeless in an alley, you hear me?!"

Winnie wasn't happy. Who could blame her? A very stressful situation arose and we all ditched her to handle it for us. But she'd done a fantastic job at the roadblock, and we were trying to give her praise, if she would stop yelling at us.

"That's fair," I replied, hands up in defensive position. "I think that's fair."

"You handled it very well," Emmaline added.

"Don't really need support from the brand-new mom, thank you very much."

"Winnifred!" I barked.

"I'm sorry," she replied.

"No," Emmaline replied, "she's right."

"Well, she's right that you're new," I replied, "but she is also right that you are her mom."

"This is adorable and I love it and I hope to see more of it," Bentley interrupted, "but we really need to keep moving here. We can assign one driver and then the rest of us can go back to celebrating the milestones of the family Sallinger."

One democratic vote later, Bentley was driving and my family was back to arguing. We'd opted to keep the refrigerated truck even though we spotted a small school bus along the side of the road.

"EVERYONE SHUT UP!" I bellowed. "Sit!" I pointed at the various spots suitable for taking a rest. "Now, I know we have our issues. Our family is really messed up, non-traditional, and confusing. We have a lot to apologize to each other for, and a lot to forgive each other for. And I'm asking you right now . . . to shove all that aside and compartmentalize that shit and pretend it doesn't exist for now . . . so that we can work together to get through this apocalypse. And if we do that, I promise—I promise—we will make room and time for all your 'prior to the end of the world' petty-ass grievances against each other."

Silence.

"Can we agree on that? Save the world first, cooperate while doing so, then argue later?"

Everyone nodded.

"Awesome!" I shouted, still pretty worked up.

Everyone was quiet for several beats.

"I'm sorry I yelled," I finally said. "I realize your mother is new to you, but she gave birth to you and was there for your first few years—both of you. You may not fully remember her, but your DNA is the same, and I'm certain you retain old memories of her love for you. The only reason she looks different or feels new to you is because she was made a prisoner of the guy we're trying to defeat right now. He used her power for his own gain and she had no choice. So while I appreciate your skepticism, I'm telling you as your father—who you *have* known all your life—that she is your mother, and her word and instruction counts as much as mine and that . . . I love her . . . and I very much remember her and have missed her for these many years."

I put out my hand and she clasped it. "We are a family, and we are going to get over all the pain eventually, and for now I just need us all to realize that . . . and act on love until we've taken this jerk down."

Bentley interrupted the love fest. "This is all excellent and edifying family stuff, I mean it, but . . . the sun is setting fast. Do we have any idea how we're planning to spend the night?"

"Where are we . . . exactly?" I asked.

"Just about fifteen miles outside of Denver's city limits," he replied.

"Huh," I muttered. "I didn't think about this earlier but . . ." I trailed off. "Bent, after Denver where are we going?"

"We continue northeast until we hit the Platte River, next state over."

"How much time do we lose if we dip down to Colorado Springs first?"

"Why would we do that?"

"Just . . . answer the question, computer-brain man!"

"A few hours at most," he admitted.

"Let's reset course to Colorado Springs. Relax, Bent, we're not going all the way there."

Twenty miles north of Colorado Springs, in the Black Forest, stood a simple log cabin. Simple, but huge—it looked to be four thousand square feet, and two stories tall.

Back when I had myself and my kids in hiding up in Canada's wilderness, I got a ping every year from my younger brother, Patrick. The ping told me his location, as well as the fact that he knew my location. It was a primitive radio version of checking up on someone. Or even stalking someone. Every couple of years we would get together, somewhere off the grid and in a different place every time.

It had been more than a year since the last ping, and more than three years since our last meet-up, but I wanted to check the location for clues, even if Patrick was no longer living there.

I rapped on the door loudly with my right hand, and in roughly one second I was dropped under the porch by a trapdoor and locked in a cage in the basement.

"Goddammit, Patrick, let me out!"

Patrick had a penchant for security—or over-security, I should say. I briefly wondered how many pizza delivery people had wound up in this very cage.

A few short minutes later I was out of the cage, out of the basement, and sitting in my brother's living room.

"You could have told me you were coming." He grinned as Freddie brought in a tray of snacks and fruits.

"We have plenty of room," Freddie smiled.

"We don't need a place to stay," I said impulsively. "We don't need snacks—though, thank you, Freddie, that is a lovely looking spread. We need help. We're on our way to rescue Bentley's kid. He's an honest-to-God Amplifier. And we need to get there before the Superintendent makes use of him to take out the moon."

I paused for five full seconds. They both looked at me funny.

"Yeah . . . dude plans to take out the moon. And I don't have to be an astronomy professor to tell you that having no moon will massively mess with our lives here on Earth. In fact, we'll have about two to three days after the moon blows up before all hell breaks loose here on Earth and everyone starts panicking, fleeing, and dying."

I paused again for emphasis.

Bentley finally joined the conversation. "Y'all wanna wrap up those snacks for us to take on the road or do you want to join the fight and come with?"

9

REINFORCEMENTS

The road trip continued to the Platte River without incident, with two new warriors gained along the way in Patrick and Freddie.

The pair had already rigged their massive cabin with "go protocols," so they piled up what they would need into our vehicle, pushed a button, and security gates and shutters closed on all the doors and windows.

"I've got cameras, too, in case anyone breaks in while we're gone," Freddie bragged.

They'd also graciously tossed several of their couch cushions into the back of the truck, which would relieve a lot of aches and pains among those of us with sore legs, arms, backs, and asses. We'd turned the refrigeration off to allow most of our party to ride in the back.

"Hopefully we won't be gone for too long," I replied.

In the back, the kids were busy reuniting with their uncle.

Though he didn't have any kids himself, my younger brother was just wonderful with my children. They adored him. He joked with them and spoke to them not as an authority figure but as a buddy. He and Winnie compared speeds racing around the back of the truck in small circles while Henry went into great detail about the growth of his powers—which he wasn't able to properly demonstrate in a moving vehicle.

"Boy, they really love him," Emmaline said.

"Yeah. I've tried hard to earn the same kind of adoration, but I think it's an uncle thing. Like, he never has to tell them to go to bed when they just wanna stay up a few more minutes or ask them to clean out the horse stalls—oh God, the animals!" I suddenly remembered the non-human farm residents that we'd just left behind to die.

"Don't worry," she assured me. "I unlocked all the barn and paddock doors and each stall inside both barns. They'll all get out. They may have to get used to eating some stuff they don't like, but they should all be fine."

"Oh, thank you! Thank you. Some of those animals were like pets to the kids. I'm so glad I can tell them that they all got out safely."

Almost as if on cue, Monster walked over and curled up next to me. He'd been busy reuniting with Patrick's bullmastiff, Leroy, a dog as loyal as he was dumb.

"You know," Em sighed, "as hard as I think you made life on those kids, I sure am impressed with their discipline. And I'm massively impressed with that farm." She shook her head in disbelief. "How did you ever get so good at farming?"

"You learn what you have to when times get hard," I replied without pausing before doubling back. "You think I made life hard on the kids?" I was defensive. Who wouldn't be? But I was also worried she was right, though I didn't realize it yet.

"I . . ." she started, before choosing her words more carefully. "I think they had a lot of responsibilities growing up." Her voice was absolutely calm, and I could tell she didn't want to argue.

But I did. Or, I thought I did.

"Those responsibilities are what taught them that discipline you so admire," I snapped—though I should state that at no point in this discussion did either of us raise our voices, and the kids were busy in the back. Freddie, who was driving, winced a few times that I could tell, but it wasn't his fault he could hear us, and we didn't have the luxury of waiting until we were alone to have every conversation.

"I don't mean to judge, Phillip," she started.

"Then don't!" I barked. "I thought you were dead. I thought you were gone forever. Our best friends had just been murdered in front of me. And I knew for a fact that custodians were being hunted, so I did what I thought was best. Went off the grid. But to do that, you have to be able to grow and hunt your own food, so I taught them how to do those things." I took a deep breath, though it was obvious I was losing steam. "I thought I was helping them. I thought I was making them stronger for the future. I . . . I did my best."

I felt her hand touching my own. "I know you did. I didn't mean to imply anything else."

"Uh, folks," Freddie called out after a few hours of general silence, "we got ourselves a police roadblock up ahead."

"Again?!" I said aloud before realizing my mistake. We'd been stopped on our way in from the west, but now we were coming in from the south. Denver was likely not covered by drones, so the roadblocks were in place in all directions. "Why didn't I think of this?!"

"Don't be so hard on yourself," Em said.

"I don't have the luxury of being easy on myself. The fate of the planet is at stake and I just made a dumbass mistake! Just . . . let me beat myself up!"

She got quiet, though I was certain the discussion was far from over.

"Alright, alright, alright," I muttered. "We'll just have Freddie drive this time and we'll all jump out of here with Emmaline's teleportation."

"I can't do it," Freddie said.

"What do you mean?" I asked. "You are literally driving right now!"

"I'm on the list, Phillip. Same as you. Same as Emmaline. Same as Patrick. We're all on the list, man. That's why we've all been in hiding!"

I looked around, knowing even as I turned my gaze that there was no answer other than the only answer, which was Winnifred. Finally I settled on her, with what I thought was a look of compassion.

"Again?" she yelled. "I barely got through it the first time! You want me to do that crap again?!"

"It's not what we want, dear," I answered, "but it is our only option—and watch your language, young lady."

"Gah!" she bellowed, "'Crap' is not a bad word!"

We had to take the chance that the Finder wasn't within five hundred miles of our location. We just had to. If any of us but Henry were caught in that van, it was all over.

So Bentley placed a tiny radio transmitter under Winnie's shirt collar and Emmaline popped us all out of the truck and up onto a nearby ridge.

From our vantage point, we could make out vehicles and human figures, but not detail. We could see the converted refrigerated truck approaching the roadblock from a half mile out.

"This is crap," the speaker crackled. "I want it on the record this is crap. This is the only time I ever wished to be the younger kid. This is such crap!"

Henry giggled.

We couldn't reply to her, of course. Hell, we were lucky Bentley even had a transmitter in his travel case so that we could hear her.

"Alright, I'm gonna shut up now so they don't see me talking to myself, but this is crap!"

From there all we heard was road noise and then the brakes as she slowed for the officer with his hands up.

There wasn't a lot of traffic on the interstates these days. There wasn't a lot of traffic on any roads these days. Sure, there were plenty of non-custodian citizens the government wasn't hunting. And there were supporters of the Superintendent; they were quite vocal and free to move about with abandon. You could usually tell them by their loudspeakers spewing propaganda or the vehicles covered in the official colors of their favorite world leader.

But so many had died in the last decade. So many had gone missing or into hiding, or had been arrested by Homeland Security—most of the custodian-related government boards and agencies that had been created throughout my lifetime had all, under the Superintendent's direction, been consolidated under Homeland Security.

Homeland Security now spent 90 percent of its allocated resources going after custodians. The other 10 percent was spent on domestic and foreign terrorists, who honestly were still surprisingly rampant. Of course, the agency just said they were protecting America from all terrorists; they didn't break down the percentages at all, because they simply redefined custodians as terrorists.

My thoughts were interrupted by the sound of the truck's window being lowered.

"Afternoon, ma'am," a male voice said. "Can I see your license?"

Registration of vehicles was no longer necessary and had died with license plates when those resources were all allocated to—you guessed it—Homeland Security. If the authorities needed to track a specific car, they did so with VIN numbers.

I imagined the disgruntled look on my daughter's face as she handed her still-fresh-from-being-printed fake ID to the officer.

"Can you tell me where you're headed?" the male voice asked.

"Denver," she replied, with not a small amount of implied "duh" in her tone.

"And what's your business in town? What's with the truck?"

She sighed. "It was the only vehicle I could find. I needed to get the hell out of Vegas after my dad kicked me out of the family once I turned eighteen and he didn't want to have to be responsible for me anymore."

It was good improv, but—

"Aw, man," Bentley sighed.

"What?" I turned.

"The ID says she's sixteen, not eighteen."

She'd gotten her own fake age wrong. In truth she was only fourteen, but we were about to find out how seriously the local cops were taking their jobs.

"Okay, ma'am," the officer replied. "Wait right here just a moment."

I guess he walked away because we heard the window going back up.

Then we heard Winnie's rapid breathing. Maybe a sniffle even. She was having a mild anxiety attack. And who could blame her? Both my kids had mild anxiety, and I would never know how much of it came from their father's genes and how much came from the bizarre and extreme lifestyle we lived.

It was probably both. Their anxiety was probably a result of both nature and nurture.

But Winnifred had been through these before, and she knew how to handle them.

"Just breathe, baby," I muttered. "You know what to do here. We've practiced a hundred times. Just breathe and count to ten. Just breathe and count to—"

"One, two," she counted, and I nearly wept for joy. "Three, four, five." Her counting was deliberate but not slow . . . it had momentum but was not fast . . . just like I'd taught her! "Six, seven—"

A loud rapping on the window jarred both Winnie and the rest of us who were eavesdropping out of our momentary slumber.

She lowered the window.

"Ma'am, can you pull over here to the right and park by those cones?"

"Um," she was concerned. "Sure. Is there something wrong, officer?"

"Just pull over there to the right by those cones," he repeated.

The engine hummed to life as we saw the truck pull up and to the right about thirty yards ahead, stopping at the orange traffic cones.

"Oh no," Emmaline said.

"Relax," I said, faking calmness. "They're always pulling people out of line for random extra checks, like at the airport."

"Shit, shit, shit, shit, shit," Winnie said softly over the radio. I guess she'd given up the pretense of using the word "crap" to annoy me. Maybe she forgot we could hear her. "What do I do? What do I do? What the hell do I do here, people? Dad? I know you can't answer, but what the hell do I do here?!"

Okay, so she knew we could hear.

I wanted so much to be able to answer her and comfort her.

"Maybe this is just random, right?" she continued, now talking herself through the situation. "Maybe they want to search the truck?"

There was a slight pause.

"Nope, nothing back there! Nothing in here incriminating. Maybe this is how they try to catch fugitives stowing away in vehicles like this? Oh, hell, we were literally carrying fugitives in this vehicle, of *course* that's what they're worried about! But why didn't they—"

Another loud rap on the window broke her train of thought. We heard the window roll down once more.

"Miss Wang?" a female voice said. "Jennifer Wang?"

"Wang?" I said out loud.

"It's the most common surname in the world," Bentley explained. "The ID maker uses a randomizer if you don't tell it what to choose for the name, so it went with the odds."

"That's me," Winnie said unconvincingly.

"At least the picture is her," Bentley defended himself. "Maybe she's adopted! It's a whole new world out there—you don't know! The last guy just glanced at it and waved her through!"

"Maybe the last guy was lazy!"

"Miss Wang," the officer continued, "can you explain to me why you were stopped at a roadblock coming into Denver from the west several hours ago, and are now being stopped coming into Denver from the south? On the same day?"

"You don't think I might have been making deliveries?" she said instantly.

God, the sarcasm on this girl was in fine form, and I know she got that from both her parents.

"I came into the city from the west with some supplies, made a delivery, then went south of town—and . . . you know . . . you guys don't have road-blocks set up for people leaving town, only those arriving, so that's why you never saw me leave . . . I made some other deliveries and it's too late for me to drive back to Vegas tonight, so I'm headed back into Denver to find a place to sleep for the night, where I will spend most of the money I just made making these stupid-ass deliveries in the first place." She paused for effect. "That sound plausible to you, ma'am?" She kind of punched the "ma'am" with an extra bit of sass.

"Oh, I like her," Emmaline whispered.

"Can you step outside the vehicle for me, ma'am?" the officer asked.

"Of course I can." Winnie made no further sound or movement.

"You better step your sassy teenage ass out of this truck right now before I pull you out!" The officer was not messing around.

I was not surprised to hear and see the van door open and Winnie step out. The officer led her toward a state police SUV, placing her in the back seat.

"Is she under arrest?" Emmaline worried.

"They didn't cuff her. No one read her any rights. She's not under arrest," Bentley assured her, "at least for now."

"One, two, three," Winnie began to count again, and I couldn't blame her for not talking to us anymore. I was glad she was so aware of her own mental health to be doing her exercises.

"Alright, they're going to take her to the nearest police station and start asking questions," I started.

"How do we keep her from talking?" Emmaline asked. "What if she tells them our plan?"

"Relax," I smiled. "She knows better."

"What?"

"Henry, you're under arrest—now tell me what you know about your sister!" I barked, as a kind of real-time demonstration.

"Screw you, I want a lawyer," he replied out of habit.

"Relax," I said again, "I trained them well."

"Alright," Em allowed, "so she knows better than to talk. Now how are we going to get her out of there?"

"That part I'm still working on," I said honestly. "It's only a matter of time before they run her DNA. And even though she's not in the system, her DNA will ping the hell out of my and Emmaline's DNA, and she'll be flagged as a custodian. This might have already happened—we don't know who else might have been waiting in that SUV," I stated for effect.

"At that point," I continued, "we have to assume the Finder will be expedited to this area. And let's be honest, we believe his powers are already being augmented by Bentley's son, the Amplifier. There is no reason to think he could not also be employing a speedster to hurry up the travel time."

There was a slight murmur as everyone processed things.

"Can't I just pop in there and save my baby?" Em begged quietly.

"Even if the Finder isn't here monitoring yet, the police are clearly interested in Winnie. You disappear her from that SUV and they are damn sure going to know custodians are hanging around this area, and that puts everyone in more danger, not just our daughter."

She nodded.

"We just don't know. And at this point, in this Denver area, we have to assume the use of powers will either be immediately detected by the Finder or detected by human cops and relayed immediately to the Finder. All of which means . . . we have to try to find a way to break Winnie out of a Denver-area jail without using any of our powers."

Another murmur, only this time more concerned, until . . .

"Well," Bentley said cheerily, "*some* of our powers are still useful. After all, I can still use mine."

10

BREAKOUT

As it turned out, they didn't take Winnie to a nearby police station; they took her to the nearest Homeland Security field office. This was both a good and bad thing.

It was good because, unlike a police station, it was not a heavily fortified building. In fact, it was a four-story medium-sized glass office building, fairly nondescript. It used to be a regional headquarters for a popular Italian food chain—it even still had paintings of tomatoes and olives hanging throughout the lobby and hallways.

It was also good because, while they did do interviews at the field office, they had no jail cells on the premises. They had a couple of "holding cells," but those had no sinks or commodes and couldn't legally house a suspect for more than a few hours. Therefore, they also had little-to-no actual guard personnel there.

A lot of DHS work was brain work—detective work, interrogations, profiling—but they typically used local city and state police for the physical end of their business, like executing warrants or working the roadblock that snared Winnie.

Her being in this building was also a bad thing, however, because this almost certainly meant that they were on to her as a likely custodian or custodian familiar. If they thought she was just a punk runaway with a fake ID, they'd have hauled her down to the local jail and contacted Child Services.

This meant they had almost certainly already run her blood test, which would tell them the names of her parents, who both happened to be pretty high up on the list of wanted suspects for these folks. Which . . . okay . . . now we *could* use our powers to rescue her and it wouldn't tip them off about her link to custodians any more than her blood had.

But also, the Finder was already surely in range and actively waiting for someone in this area to use their powers, which would put us all at risk.

The sound of a door slamming snapped through the speaker, then footsteps. A metal chair being pulled back along a concrete floor, slowly, for maximum screeching noise. Then a muffled sound, and finally a voice.

"I'm gonna give you a chance to come clean here," the voice said. It sounded like a man, mid-fifties maybe, not kind but not mean. "Go on and tell me the truth and we can make sure you don't end up in any trouble yourself."

"Bullshit," I barked as I climbed the steps toward the roof of the Mega Jon's Mega Ton Sporting Goods store across the street from the DHS building.

"Keep off the radio so we can listen," Bentley reminded me.

He was the least mobile of all of us, so we set him up in the actual escape vehicle—a DHS van. There were dozens of them just parked in the parking lot, like a rental car fleet with no customers, as though every employee was job-required to drive a black windowless van to work every day. Anyway, no one would look twice at such a vehicle, which made it an excellent hiding place.

We were using a modified version of the old rig Henry and I had used back in high school—my implanted eyes were capable of broadcasting a feed over the air a certain distance. So Bentley just created a magnified receiver to pick that signal up, and he was then able to see everything I could see, even when I switched to infrared or night vision.

He was also tapped into the security cameras inside the Homeland Security building as well as nearby buildings and traffic and security camera feeds.

Back in the interrogation room, Winnie said nothing in reply to the officer. I was so scared and yet so proud.

The man sighed. "Why don't we just start with your real name," he said, bargaining like a true classic "good cop," making himself trustworthy by drastically lowering the bar right out of the gate. "We know it's not Jennifer Wang."

"She's good," Bentley said. "She hasn't flinched. Hasn't even looked up."

Bentley had video, courtesy of his hack of the building, which he had described as "child's play thirty years ago, let alone today"; the DHS was going so hard after custodians they couldn't even conceive of anyone coming after them. Anyway, the rest of us only had audio.

I would have visuals soon, by virtue of my extra perceptive eyeball abilities, but not until I got into position. "That's my girl," I said, smiling as I continued to climb.

"You in position yet?" Bentley asked.

"Not yet. Close. Close enough . . . go ahead and check on everyone for mission status," I replied as I finally reached the roof-access door and opened it, stepping out into the crisp evening air.

"Why don't you just come clean," the officer said before dropping what he thought would be a bomb, ". . . Winnifred?"

But Winnie had been trained for this kind of thing, at least through discussion. She understood that she had a right to a lawyer but that the right to counsel might be overlooked by aggressive officers. She knew that a blood test would reveal her true identity, so she definitely wasn't surprised to hear her real first name.

"Why don't you go ahead and tell me your real name. We already know it. What's your real name?" He was taunting her.

Finally my daughter's voice came through the earpiece as she responded, "Last name *Lawyer*, first name *I Want My*."

I laughed.

"Does she even have a lawyer?" Emmaline asked.

"Copy," Bentley replied to me. "Mission Control, ops status check, please await your call sign to reply; I know some of you are rusty, so we are checking radio by call sign then mission ready status. Here we go . . . Eagle."

"Check," I replied as I reached the edge of the wall designated as my position. "Mission GO."

"Dog One," Bentley barked next.

"Check," Patrick replied. "Mission GO."

"Dog Two," Bent continued.

"Check, mission GO," my youngest replied.

I figured if my son was going to be involved in the mission to rescue his sister, and I had to be up on a roof somewhere else, I wanted my brother near him to keep him safe. The fact that they both had dogs only sealed their pairing.

"Damsel," Bentley said, a smile in his voice.

"You really enjoy calling me that, don't you?" Emmaline replied. "And check. And mission GO."

"Explosives."

"Check, mission GO," Freddie replied.

That's everybody, I thought.

"That's everybody," Bentley announced. "Mission is GO on my command."

And then we waited.

"That's cute," the officer said. "Do you even know the name of a lawyer?"

"Matlock, Perry Mason, Matt Murdock, Keanu Reeves in that Devil movie—"

As a pop-culture fan, the father in me was very proud at her reply.

The officer was less impressed and slammed his fists down on the table . . . at least that's what it sounded like. "Is this a joke to you?!"

"Clearly," she laughed.

"Oh, I like her," Emmaline repeated herself.

"Yeah, you like her when she's doing this to fascist cops, but you wouldn't enjoy it when you're just asking her to take out the trash," I responded.

"I never got the chance to ask her to take out the trash," she countered.

"And whose fault is that?" I said without really thinking it through.

"It's not mine!" she responded.

"Can we do radio silence on our end until mission GO?" Bentley barked, clearly not enjoying our latest outburst.

For several seconds there was complete silence on the radio. I heard the faint sound of cars going by below every now and then. Again, life still went on in America, but at half the speed . . . half the population . . . half the everything. Sometimes less.

Finally, I spoke. "You mean complete radio silence or just mostly radio—"

"Will you shut up?!" Bentley screamed.

"I gotcha. I hear you," I backpedaled.

"What if I told you we know who your mother and father are?" the officer asked. He was still pretty casual with most of his deliveries.

"I already know, so it wouldn't surprise me much," she replied. "I mean, unless I was adopted and my real parents are super fascinating rich Swiss banker-types with a lavish mansion and a stable of hunting dogs. That would be pretty rad, honestly," she added.

"Oh, Winnie," I breathed into the open mic by accident.

"She's doing just fine," Patrick replied. "Stalling him expertly."

"Yeah, by antagonizing him. Everyone has a breaking point," I explained nervously.

"We're close enough to GO I don't think it will matter," Pat replied.

"I could have ordered mission GO in the last twenty seconds while you guys were talking and no one would have heard it because no one is observing radio silence!" Bentley ranted.

Everyone laughed, and everyone went out of their way to push the button to open their mic to the channel so that Bentley could hear them laughing.

When the laughter died, Bentley spoke. "I hope you all got that out of your system, and I hope you remember your roles because GO GO GO, mission GO. MISSION GO NOW!"

He wasn't trying to surprise us. Bentley had the video camera view of everything big and small in this operation, from the building we were breaching to the escape route. Only he knew what our options looked like, and so we trusted him, and the mission began.

"Explosives, stand by," Bentley said clearly. "Dogs . . . Go!"

Dog One and Dog Two had identical missions, just from opposite ends of the building. The goal was for each to enter the building, with their dog, and then get entangled together near the customer service desk.

This would create the first layer of diversion we felt we needed. There were some personnel throughout the building that would take notice of or be alerted to a disturbance in the lobby, from security staff to other building management types.

Ahead of the two dog decoys, Bentley had already sent Emmaline into the building and up the elevator to the fourth floor where Winnifred was being questioned.

Em's mission excuse? She'd just managed to escape a volatile and abusive relationship and her boyfriend had turned out to be connected to a terrorist cell that was actively planning an event in the Denver area.

That story got her whisked to the top floor in no time, with dozens of agents heading off to search her home and place of work—both of those places were faked, of course, and I do feel bad for the unsuspecting family at 119 Elizabeth St. W. and the entire Taco Tony's payroll . . . but everything got sorted out and those folks were eventually compensated.

Now the entire building was in a frenzy over either the lobby insanity or the hot new terrorism lead. Even the officer interrogating Winnie had stepped out to see what the commotion was about.

And that meant it was time for Freddie's payload to play its part.

"Freddie," Bentley said softly into the radio, "time to blow."

A quarter mile away stood a vacant office tower . . . eight stories. It once housed the good people of the Everyday Bountifuls brand—they made intensely sugared fruit drinks and had gone out of business four years prior.

"Copy," Freddie replied.

A moment later the entire DHS building shook violently, as though an earthquake had just occurred underneath it. However, it was quickly determined that an explosion had taken place north of the building.

Before anyone could recover or gather a thought, another explosion in the same area rocked the property again.

The building then emptied faster than a fire drill, as every available officer raced to the scene of the second, more powerful explosion. Some went on foot, but dozens raced to the parking lot and chose company vans to drive to the location even faster.

Bentley watched the chaos unfold around him, until suddenly an unexpected turn of events occurred. It was something we hadn't accounted for or even dreamed might happen during our plan.

Knock, knock, knock. Someone rapped on the van's window.

"Open up!" barked a soldier in full riot gear, a handful of others behind him. "Let's go! Terrorists just blew up a building, let's fucking go!"

Bentley pressed the button that opened the van's side door, and special forces soldiers piled inside.

"Alright, we are on the second floor, making our way to the exit point. Bentley, time to move."

That was Emmaline and Winnie, following the plan and completely unaware that Bentley and his van had been compromised.

"Bentley?"

But there was only silence.

11

THE RIVER

"Um," I breathed.

"Why isn't Bentley responding?!" Em said, finishing my thought.

"It looks like he's been commandeered. A bunch of SWAT-type guys jumped into the van and it drove off! I don't know!"

"Nope, nope," came Bentley's voice. It was a relief to hear it. "I got out with my hands up—told them I was just delivering the van from the shop."

Oh, thank God, I thought.

"Oh, thank God," I said out loud.

"We still have a problem, though," Bentley continued. "We don't have a getaway vehicle anymore. All the other DHS vans are gone too! I'm just . . . standing here in the tree line hoping no one spots me!"

"If they took all the vehicles then no one is going to spot you," I answered. "I'm sure we can find another vehicle."

"You're the one with the altitude," he responded.

"Right," I realized. "Hang on a sec." I scampered over to the northeast corner. "Okay. Let's see here . . . now . . . amplify." My artificial eyes were superior to regular eyes in every way. They not only gave me thermal and night vision, but they also had an amplification ability to up to five times what the normal eye could see. And they responded to voice commands.

"Zoom and enhance!" Patrick yelled over the radio joyously.

"Everyone head over to Bentley's position—Em, Pat, Win, Hen—you copy?"

Four quick "copy"s followed.

"Okay." I began facing northeast and spun in a slow circle, calling out possible vehicles as I went. "I see a school bus parked at Walmart—that's no good. There's a camper there as well, but I see at least six heat signatures inside. Occupado." I spun a bit more. "There's a city bus over here on lunch break or something, not moving. Not sure I want to steal a city bus . . . that could have a tracking system and many are electric these days without much range."

I spun some more, not seeing anything really good for a group of our size until . . .

"Okay, here's a church van, parked next to the church, no one around for blocks. That van is unguarded."

"I don't know," Emmaline replied. "Stealing from a church? Seems a bit . . . foul."

"Well, we are going to have to do some foul stuff if we hope to actually stave off this apocalypse, but . . . I agree . . . stealing from a church is probably a bit too far," I replied.

"Just . . . for the record," Bentley added, "I have no problem stealing from a church. In case it ever comes up again."

"A cement truck . . . a UPS truck . . . some kind of bachelorette SUV limo thing . . . I don't know, man. There aren't a lot of good options out here," I admitted.

"Uh, guys," a new voice joined the radio chat. It was Freddie. "I'm walking away from that explosion everyone is talking about," he said, referring to the explosion he himself had caused. "Well, as I leave the scene, I'm encountering *lots* of empty vehicles . . . vans and trucks, DHS and EMS . . . all abandoned since their occupants ran into the fire to try to save people . . . I don't know . . . why don't I just get in one of these things and drive away? Come pick you guys up and we go along?"

We were all silent for a good five or six seconds as the obviousness of his message sunk in.

"Um," I started. "Um . . . yeah, let's do that!"

"Agreed," Bentley chimed in. "Honestly, I can see the two dog handlers *and* Emmaline and Winnifred right now. They're close. Phillip . . . time to use the zip-line."

"I can't just run down the stairs?"

"Only if you want all of us sitting here in the vehicle for ten minutes while law enforcement swarms on the ground and in the air."

"So no?"

"No!" Bentley barked. "Unless you wanna use your powers, which would actually be faster but you seem pretty dead-set against, jump now, you idiot!"

I didn't love heights for most of my life, but I'd grown even more wary since I'd stopped using my powers. A good fall was a good way to die. I hoped to avoid falls.

I decided to trust a friend I'd given up on trusting years ago, if only because I didn't see a faster way off this roof. So I slapped the metal "belt" around the corded wire, took a deep-ass breath, and jumped.

It was a thrilling ride, though I'll never admit it.

Despite the "bombing incident," as it was currently being referred to on the local news, it was surprisingly easy for Freddie to steal a DHS van and drive it out of the area without anyone looking twice.

Chaos is a criminal's best friend. That's why you always see them causing diversions in the movies. Diversions create chaos.

As far as anyone paying attention was concerned, we were a DHS crew in a DHS vehicle on our way to DHS business that was obviously very important.

The vehicle had its pros and cons. It was full of gasoline—yay. But it had a DHS tracking system embedded in its software—boo. But Bentley was able to hack the vehicle programming and disable the tracking device—yay. Unfortunately, disabling the tracking device would be noticed by DHS and they would begin looking for the vehicle—boo. However, we still had a nice stash of space blankets, and we could paper the outside of the car with them to avoid detection by satellites and drones—yay. But we'd still be susceptible to radar—boo.

Ultimately it was decided that DHS didn't have much use for radar, since it was less useful the closer you got to the ground. But we also didn't want to take the vehicle all the way to North Platte. If the feds found the van abandoned in that small municipality, they'd know for sure we made for the river.

We took it halfway until we found a fairly busy truck stop. It only took us about two hours to find someone to swap vehicles with. That surprised me, until I remembered the kinds of people that were left alive and still traveling during all this nonsense: survivors, some more desperate than others.

In exchange for our large van, low on gas, which could avoid detection by satellite and drone, we received a station wagon with heavily tinted windows. It smelled like pot.

We couldn't afford to be choosy, and Pot Wagon Guy could sense it, so we traded straight up and got absolutely dunked on the value, except for one important area: the wagon was full of gas.

So, I drove the wagon and everyone else took turns complaining about how uncomfortable they were for the remainder of the drive, like we weren't supposed to sacrifice while trying to save the world.

You expected a red carpet? Servants with grapes?

Eventually we hit the town of North Platte, which had three main docks along the Platte River. We weren't exactly here to buy or rent, so we did our best to stay quiet as we walked along the pier. Eventually we found an ideal vehicle, a medium motorboat named *Bagpipe Betty*. She was currently raised up out of the water, for protection during the colder season. The logs showed she hadn't been out to sea in nearly four months, and there was more than enough room for all of us aboard.

Bentley did a sweep for homing beacons, and found none, and so it was that we all set quiet sail aboard the SS *Bagpipe Betty*, hoping for safe waters all the way to our next destination, which we hoped was south of Omaha, connecting to the Missouri River.

"You must hate me."

After checking on the kids below, and finding them sound asleep, with Bentley driving and Freddie and Patrick bunked and hunkered down there with the kids and the dogs, Em and I finally had a chance to talk.

We sat on the front edge of the boat as it puttered along. We had years to catch up on, and hours to do it in.

"Why would I hate you?" she asked.

I lowered my gaze away from hers. "I . . . I screwed up our kids, I think. Like . . . I don't think I've been a very good father. And I gave up on you instantly . . . I never even considered it was a faked death and that you might still be alive . . . I just bought it completely!" I started heaving and sobbing as I spoke, and quickly clammed up as tears rolled down my face.

"You did the best you could, honey," she said softly. "You couldn't have known I was alive. And everything you did was intended to keep our kids safe, and that's impressive and laudable! I'm actually so in awe of you right now. You didn't bend or buckle. You just carved out a life that would let your kids grow and learn in safety . . . You need to let that insecurity go, Phillip," she urged.

My sobbing continued, despite knowing how right she was.

But she was undeterred. "We're at the end, baby. This is apocalypse-type shit going on. The Superintendent wants to blow up the moon in addition to killing all custodians! If we don't work together, everyone dies. The planet dies. Your children die. I *need* you to snap out of it and get with me on this, babe!"

I heard her. And thus I began to slow my breathing. I counted to ten quietly in my head. A process I repeated over and over. Em was patient, waiting with me through every breath.

"You're right," I replied, finally. "I shouldn't have gotten emotional."

"Phillip," she instantly responded, "I'm thrilled you got emotional. It shows me you're still the man I fell in love with, one who is fiercely protective of close family and friends. We just need the emotions to wait a bit. I know it's hard for you with the anxiety, and I won't ask you to take on more than you can bear, but . . . for now . . ." she trailed off.

"I know."

She kissed me on the forehead and I returned the gesture.

We were interrupted by the sound of a jet engine about to pass by overhead.

No, wait, that's not right, I thought to myself. *Helicopter? No. Train?* My chest was rumbling. *Oh no!* I looked up and to the southeast.

There it was. Unmistakable. It was a rocket, headed into space, and I knew the destination immediately: the moon.

The Superintendent had finally launched his missile.

He'd long been stoking the fires of custodian hate by implying that superheroes on Earth got their powers from the moon. Even as he sent death squads around the country to capture and kill custodians, he continued to promise the endgame was the moon.

Apparently, he wasn't bluffing.

"Is that what I think it is?" Em asked softly.

"That," I replied, "is the end of the world."

12

THE MOON

"Ladies and gentlemen. Servicemembers around the world. Patriots and defenders of the Constitution. All our hardworking DHS members and their families, millions strong . . . to every God-fearing American in listening range . . . good evening."

It was the Superintendent, going live—audio-only for us—after the launch of the missile. He had gone live less than thirty minutes after the launch, in fact.

"He knew everyone would see it, so he had to address it," Freddie said, stating the obvious.

"Tonight," the voice continued, "I have authorized the use of excessive force in order to stop the most dangerous enemy on our planet—the custodian. The custodian pretends to guard while he—or she—instead polices and restricts, making up policy on the fly. They want to be heroes, but they are the only ones allowed to define who the criminals are. They want permission to destroy third-party property in the pursuit of so-called criminals and they want absolution from criminal prosecution in the act thereof."

He paused a good five beats.

"And I WILL NOT TOLERATE IT!" he finally bellowed.

Even quietly coasting on this dark river, we could hear cheers ring out among the hills and towns surrounding us. The Superintendent was quite popular . . . at least with those citizens he'd left alive.

No one on the boat spoke, though we were all awake and listening intently. We'd been on the boat since we hit the Platte River, as planned, but many among us were still adjusting to the ebbs and flows of the water-bound lifestyle.

Bentley kept glancing at the rocket, then the moon, then doing some doodle math; then he'd repeat the process.

"How fast is it going?" I asked quietly against the white noise of the droning on of the Superintendent's speech.

"Faster than previously considered possible," he replied, still doing calculations. "That's all I know for now."

"Do you think he used your son's powers to create a faster or more powerful rocket?"

"Yes, I do," he said in a way that was hauntingly resolute.

"We have done so many studies we are overrun with results," the Superintendent continued over the radio. "Every single test comes back the same: These so-called 'heroes' are getting their powers from the moon. Yes, our moon. Earth's moon." He paused for effect. "Is it really so surprising? The same moon that controls our planet's ocean tides and determines the length of our days . . . is it so shocking that same entity could add power to those humans susceptible to it?"

"This is insanity," Winnifred said. "He's just making stuff up!"

"Politicians have been making stuff up for longer than even I've been alive," I replied before couching things by adding, "though it's never been quite this bad."

"Do people out there really believe this?" Henry asked.

"Unfortunately, son, they do," I answered.

"A lot of them do," Emmaline reinforced.

"Smaller percentage of the overall public did before he massacred a bunch of heroes, but still . . ." I tossed in at the last second, much to Em's chagrin. She shook her head at me.

"And so tonight, fellow patriots, I have authorized the firing of the most advanced weapon ever created. It launched just over half an hour ago, it is aimed directly at the moon, and it will deliver its historic payload in less than twenty-four hours." The radio sparkled with the sound of the cheering crowds around the world being piped into the broadcast.

A collective sigh went up from the boat.

"If I ever meet this guy, I'm gonna staple his lips shut," Freddie grumped.

Now we had a timeline. One day until the moon exploded. After that . . . it was all speculation, of course.

"Why can't we stop it?" Henry begged. He was old enough to understand the implications of the missile, but young enough to think it was an easy fix.

"It's moving too fast," I replied.

"Winnie can move fast!" he countered. "Uncle Pat can move fast!"

"It's not just that," I relented. "A human can only survive in space for a handful of seconds, and we don't have anyone powerful enough to stop it."

"Even you?" he asked, doe-eyed.

"Even me."

"Aren't you strong enough? I heard you whipped a train around like a rope!" Winnie argued.

"I did. I did," I replied. "But a static train isn't anything like a rocket being propelled as fast as this one is. I can't stop this rocket, kids, I'm sorry. I used to be strong, and maybe I still am, but this rocket is unstoppable."

"Even with Bentley's brains?" Henry countered. "He's computer smart, no?"

I laughed before quickly settling and calmly replying, "He is computer smart, but no one can spend more than a dozen seconds up there in space without a suit, and there's just no way for Bentley to learn the missile's software fast enough to alter it in that short amount of time. And that's assuming we're now willing to just use our powers and expose our position . . . because even if we did send Emmaline and Bentley up there on a mission, the rest of us would be sitting ducks right here on the river."

"So we just have to sit here floating down the freaking Platte River while we watch our moon get exploded?" Freddie asked.

"Yeah," I replied.

"Correction," Bentley offered. "We have just crossed from the Platte River to the Missouri River."

There was a long, tired pause.

"But we're still screwed regarding the moon?" Freddie barked.

"Yeah, no," Bentley begged, "I can't do anything about the moon, man."

Where were you when the moon exploded?

I began to realize this would become a common form of expression in the future, should humanity even survive.

I was on a river, trying to get to the nation's capital to rescue a hostage. That would be my answer. And I wasn't super pleased with it.

Daylight arrived before the missile made impact. Few of us had slept.

Everything about life had been turned upside-down, whether you were a human, a custodian, an anti-custodian, or just a regular animal. The world was never going to be the same, and it seemed as though everyone got the sense of that truth around the same time.

"We still have work to do," Bentley barked.

We'd pulled off to the river's edge to rest and have lunch, but it seemed he was raring to get back on the water.

No one moved.

"What's going to happen?" I asked on behalf of everyone.

Bentley seemed eager to move on, which meant that the answer was probably unfortunate. But I wanted to know, and so did everyone else.

"Bentley," I said, softly, "talk to us about what happens when the moon explodes."

He sighed heavily, turned, and sat down.

Almost on cue, we all sat down ourselves, most of us on the ground.

"We don't know. Nobody knows," he opened. "Everything depends on the payload of that weapon—which we don't know—and the effect it will have on the moon, which we also don't know. There are too many scenarios to count."

"Give us the most likely," I said, kind but firm.

"Best-case scenario? Nothing much changes. The moon turns to powder as it's obliterated. Our days would fix firmly on twenty-four hours each— that number moves bit-by-bit right now because of the moon's pull on our circulation. We'd have . . . a lot better view of the night sky and all the stars and the Milky Way."

"Sounds pretty awesome," Henry said, speaking what most of us were thinking.

"The dust might form cool Saturn-type rings around Earth."

"I'd buy a ticket to that," Freddie replied.

Everyone seemed delighted by that notion.

"Or the dust could cover the planet in a cloud, blocking us from the sun."

Everyone's mood suddenly soured.

"Worst-case scenario?" Bentley continued. "It breaks into huge chunks, one or more of which fall to Earth. The speed of impact would be less than a typical asteroid, of course, but the sheer size of the moon chunks would cause things like tsunamis a mile high, continental fires, nuclear winter, basically. Maybe ten thousand survive . . . on a global scale. And they won't survive long with no way to grow or hunt for food."

"Jesus," I breathed.

"Middle of the road? A mix of both, probably," Bentley said, almost cheerily—it wasn't that he was happy about the news, but happy about his intellect allowing him to be of help to the group. "Some medium-sized lunar chunks hit the Earth, cause some localized massive damage but the planet as a whole isn't terribly affected. The smaller chunks would likely burn up in the atmosphere or float off into space."

"That sounds . . . kind of cool . . . maybe?" my son said, still wrestling with the new reality of this world.

"But in all three scenarios . . . indeed in any scenario . . . the loss of the moon tilts the Earth's axis a considerable degree, to the point that polar ice caps would melt and flood continents as well as sending ice ages to places like Brazil and the French Riviera. And our orbit around the sun starts shrinking. It's the current climate crisis on steroids."

Everyone stayed silent while processing this information.

Bentley finally summarized, "So once the moon explodes, we have somewhere between a few days and a few decades, maybe a few centuries . . . but Earth is fucked either way, which . . . was kind of always the case, but whatever. Now it's faster. Anyway, in the meantime let's go rescue my son, eh?"

"We deal with the problems one at a time, each as they threaten us most. For now, that's still Bentley's kidnapped kid."

"I want it on record that I suggested we split up," Patrick called out.

"What record?" I replied. "Look around, Pat. No one is taking notes. This isn't a city council meeting; this is the end of the world!"

"Then shouldn't we address more than one crisis?" he replied. And he was right. But I didn't want to admit it. He continued, "If we can't find Bentley's kid, I don't think we can do anything about the moon crisis, because none of us are strong enough. And if we can't fix the moon crisis, I don't think it matters whether or not we find Bentley's kid!"

I was quietly proud of my brother's reasoning skills. He took after me, of course.

"We started down this path to save Graham Crittendon," I barked. "We *will* save this kid—that's the mission! That's the only mission until we know what this missile does to the moon. Discussing it now is just premature."

"Prematurely discussing possible disasters is what some people call planning." I was surprised and a little hurt to realize the voice was Emmaline's. "We can go full steam ahead to save him while still planning for contingencies. I mean, Jesus, Phillip, look at us . . . we're on a boat right now. Why can't we use this time to plan various alternate plans for how the moon might explode?"

"You're right," I relented. "We can plan for both events simultaneously." Under my breath I added, "Be careful what you wish for."

13

EVEN MORE DETOURS

The Superintendent was surrounded by security personnel at all times. When he slept, when he ate, when he went to McBryan's for a Big Bryan with extra mayo, when he urinated, when he watched his girlfriends play tennis. There was no "getting to" a man like this.

And because he was a world leader, the location of the Superintendent was largely public knowledge. We could know where he was, and even often where he was going to be, just by watching the White House schedule released to the media or watching TV.

Getting him alone, though, would be next to impossible.

So the rescue options were quite limited.

First, we had to find the jerk. Then, we'd have to use Emmaline to jump in, grab Graham, and jump back out. *Then*, we'd need a way to disappear or outrun the agents and vehicles of the most highly funded federal agency in the history of the United States with most of their drones and satellites after us.

And even if we did all that, we'd still have a moon crisis to address.

For now, most of us slept as we slid down the Missouri River toward the great Mississippi. The waters would then be rough enough to require us to take turns standing watch; if the Missouri River was a house cat, the Mississippi was a lion.

"What are they like?" my wife asked.

We were once again seated in the front of the ship—the bow? Like I give a shit. We were once again trying to make up for ten years of lost time.

"They're so amazing, Em," I replied honestly. "Winnie is . . . well, she's wicked fast. I think she's already faster than Patrick, but I'll never tell him that."

Em laughed.

"She's so smart. It's like once she learns a thing it never leaves her brain. I quiz them every night, and Henry seems to have a pretty normal recall time, but Winnie . . . she just answers immediately like a robot."

"You quiz them every night?" She wasn't being aggressive. And yet, the question itself seemed to attack my own parenting style.

"I did before we left our farm, yeah." I paused. I was confused with her apparent disapproval. "I gave them each regular chores to keep up a private farm in a time when custodians were being hunted! I was just creating responsibility and a routine."

She took a deep breath. "I don't want to fight. I shouldn't have asked in such an argumentative manner."

"I don't want to fight either." I stopped for a moment and tried to consider what it might be like to be away from your family for ten years and then suddenly return to them. "I was probably too hard on them," I finally admitted, as much to myself as to my wife. "I just wanted to raise them strong and fearless and full of knowledge . . . while also keeping them off the radar of the DHS."

"You did so well," Em replied. "They have so much of both of us in them. I'm glad they have so much knowledge. I'm glad you hid them from evil. But I still think they missed out on some stuff."

"Yeah."

"I think they're severely lacking in peer relationships."

"What was I supposed to do, take them to the local teen groups and risk—"

"I didn't say you did anything wrong. The kids can be lacking in certain experiences without it meaning you messed up, Phillip. Frankly—and I don't mean this to be rude—but . . . frankly, I'm amazed you not only kept the family alive, but you provided an environment for them to thrive."

She smiled again—a sight still so new to me I grinned ear to ear; I had only received my eye implants a few months before she'd been killed—or, as it turned out, kidnapped. "I can wish they'd had more without it meaning that I think you messed up. Just as I can love you while seeing your flaws, I can appreciate what you did right raising these kids while I was gone and also point out areas you may have fallen short."

"Oh, I like her," Winnie whispered to the eavesdropping Henry, not realizing that even though my eyes were new and powerful, my hearing was still top-notch.

"Me too," Hen replied.

I'd have barked at them for listening in, but I was too pleased to hear such affection for their mother, who, to them, was still largely a stranger.

Monster's ears perked up, but he was tired and his ears deemed the whispered conversation to be harmless.

The mighty Mississippi lived up to her name and we went booming downriver, making good time. Such good time that we'd stopped again along a large bank to rest and eat.

The kids were tired of eating cold food and wanted to start a fire. I'd objected, but Bentley reminded me that a lot of the Superintendent's fans and supporters were camping people . . . people who rejected the city in favor of more rural living.

"There are probably fires all along this river right now. There's no reason to think a campfire arouses suspicion."

"Except for the fact that we're being hunted."

"They don't have any idea where we are, Phillip," he said warmly. "It's fine."

Reluctantly, I nodded.

Immediately Patrick and Winnifred began a spontaneous speed-battle to see who could gather firewood the fastest, while Henry beelined for the supply basket to pick out the canned goods he wanted to warm up for dinner.

"You know," Bentley said as he lowered himself down onto a log I had just set in place near the site of the impending fire, "maybe we're going about this the wrong way."

I tossed another log next to his, and then two more along the edge. "How do you mean?" I gestured to Emmaline to sit, but she shook her head and pointed at the river's edge, indicating she was going to go join Freddie, who was desperately trying to catch some kind of fish for dinner. I just nodded.

Monster got up and trudged along after her. We hadn't had Monster when we "lost" Emmaline, so it was cute to see him taking to her so quickly. Dogs have amazing senses and instincts, and I was sure he was just taking his cues from me; if I loved her, he loved her.

"We're in hiding right now, basically," Bentley continued.

"Other than the fire," I pointed out like a jerk.

"Other than the fire," he mimicked. "The point is . . . we believe they're after us, no?"

"We do," I concurred. I heard the buzzing and whizzing of my brother and oldest child dropping off firewood and heading back out for another armful.

"And we think they're using this Finder person to do it?"

"If we use our powers, the Finder would know, if he or she were in range, yes."

"And the range is expanded, we believe," Bentley said.

"Yeah." I began to wonder if he was talking to me or just to himself. Like, did my responses here even matter?

"But the range can only be expanded if my son is near the Finder, right? He's the one that amplifies the abilities. And if the Finder *and* my son are both out here looking for us . . ."

"Then maybe the Superintendent is out here too!" I blurted out, simply certain I'd discovered Bentley's point.

"Forget the Superintendent," he replied, dashing my hopes with a wave of his hand. "He's nothing. He could be in Aruba."

"Why would he go to Aruba and leave behind the super powerful Amplifier kid that helps him control his kingdom?"

"Because," Bentley stated, trying to be patient, "he likely has enough custodians on his payroll, as well as fancy military jets, that he can get where he needs to be within moments or, at most, hours. My point is this: We *were* going to go after the Superintendent in order to find my son . . . that's backward. We need to go after my *son's* location, regardless of where that asshole dictator is. We don't even need to see that guy if we don't want to. We just need my kid."

"And then we have to solve the moon thin—"

"With my kid we can solve the moon thing!"

I was taken aback by his shouting, but still replied. "Curious how we're going to achieve that, but okay, let's say you're right. Let's say your kid isn't with the Superintendent."

"The Superintendent does not matter!" he bellowed.

"Right, sorry," I was still meek, but tossed in a bit of attitude because I was sure Bent would eventually realize he went a little too hard at me during this conversation. "So your kid is out here, with the Finder and probably a lot of military and DHS folks, looking for us. Is that your theory?"

"Correct."

Henry interrupted as he walked up. "Okay, I got green beans, white beans, and a couple kinds of corn," he blurted, dumping the cans on the ground, oblivious to the conversation at hand. "Hope you guys are good with those."

"Four cans for seven people?" I turned quickly and asked.

"Aw, man," Henry said, realizing he had more work to do before stomping away.

"Alright, so how do we find him? How do we track the Finder—a custodian who tracks the use of powers, mind you. How do we track the tracker?"

"I think," Bentley smiled, "if you listen to yourself, you might find the answer."

A whoop went out from the shore, a likely effect of Freddie having caught a fish. I glanced back to see Emmaline clapping and Monster running in little happy circles.

I went back over my own statement in my mind and still couldn't find the answer. My face must have registered a humorous confusion, because Bentley started giggling. "I don't get it," I said. "I don't know what I said that is so important."

"A custodian who tracks the use of powers, mind you," he said, parroting my own words back at me, helping me connect the dots.

"You can't be serious," I breathed.

"Why go looking for someone who is already looking for us?" He grinned at his own brilliance.

"You're out of your mind," Freddie repeated for the third time.

"You want to intentionally draw all the bad guys directly to our location?!" Emmaline yelled.

It had been a tense meal of bass and overheated canned vegetables as Bentley laid out his logic and everyone took turns stepping all over it.

"I do." He was smiling. It wasn't a cocky smile, or an argumentative one. He wasn't trolling. This was a smile of the absolute zen of confidence. I had only seen it a few times.

"Graham is with the Finder," I said to no one in particular. "If the Finder comes here, so will Graham." I was trying to find a flaw, but there didn't seem to be one.

"Great, so then once we grab the kid—which sounds super easy, by the way," Freddie spat sarcastically, "how the hell do we get away from all the tanks and planes and soldiers and guns?"

"The fish is really tasty," Winnie said, trying to tamp down the conversational flames.

"I think we're all overlooking an easy solution to that problem," Bentley responded, before turning to look directly at my wife, who had to stop eating mid-spoonful of corn.

"What?" she garbled, her mouth full of food.

"The final power we use during this event drawing these people to our location will be Emmaline's power of teleportation. And as long as she teleports us outside of a five-hundred-mile range of our position, they won't have any idea where we've gone."

"That's assuming the satellites don't pick us up," Patrick countered.

"You leave the satellites to me," Bentley smiled.

"Seems like we're leaving an awful lot of our survival to you, though."

"Pat," I growled.

"What?" he came back instantly. "This guy was a straight up *villain* last time we saw him, and now most of our plan to save the day is resting on *his* discretion! Seriously?"

"I'm sorry, Patrick," Bentley said evenly. "I am sorry about my past mistakes. And I'm sorry that this plan currently is mine. I assure you that no one is more in hero mode than I am when the mission is to RESCUE MY KIDNAPPED SON!" He breathed loudly and heavily for a few beats.

Everyone looked around. No one wanted to speak next. Except for Patrick.

"I just hope you're still a good teammate after we get him back, because we'll still need your help."

After a long, deep breath, Bentley finally answered. "I will be. I assure you all I'm not the man I was seventeen years ago, but I'll continue to prove it as needed."

Patrick leaned in toward Bentley, staring him down for several beats. "Good enough for me." He extended his hand, and Bentley shook it.

"So what now?" I asked, chuckling at the recently relieved tension.

"Now," Bentley said, "we need a plan . . . and a little bit of research and reconnaissance."

14

FLIP IT

The missile—powered by the combined abilities of the Fireballer and Bentley's son, the Amplifier—finally struck the moon that night, though from Earth the process seemed to be happening in slow motion. Universe time appears slow to us only because our own time is so fast . . . because we are so infinitesimally tiny, not to mention relatively insignificant in the grand scheme of things.

Everyone gaped and gawked for a long while, until it became obvious that the movement of the explosion was so slow. You could see it moving, but it was oddly glacial to our eyes.

And it was still too soon to know how dramatic the impact would be and how many pieces, big or small, would remain of our lunar satellite.

St. Louis was behind us, and Memphis in front of us . . . but we were no longer bound by the river or our original course to Washington, DC, now that the objective was to bring the enemy to us.

So we debated where to make our stand, even as we floated down the roaring Mississippi.

"We have to choose someplace remote," Bentley insisted. "There could be collateral damage if this becomes a fight. We can't risk innocent people getting hurt."

"*If* this becomes a fight?" Emmaline asked. But the conversation rolled on without her.

"That's all well and good, but I am more concerned about where we plan to go next . . . then we pick a place to have this 'fight' based on our next move," I countered.

"Yeah," Bentley agreed. "We need to do both. We need to find a location for this thing that serves all our needs."

"So where do we go after we have Graham back in our custody?" Patrick asked. "Where can we be safe and keep him from another attempted grab?"

Bentley and I locked eyes. There was a bit of searching there, for both of us.

"I, for one, can't let things end at saving Graham," I finally said. I looked up at the still-exploding moon. For now, there appeared to be three larger chunks breaking up, as well as a lot of dust. Cracks appeared here and there on the three large pieces, leading us to speculate that they might break up even more as they shot away from the explosion site. The moonlight was already becoming a sort of fractal weird version of its usual self, shining down like different-sized spotlights, with patches of the ground in shadow . . . untouched by it as the moon split apart.

"I've been hidden for years," I continued. "I've ignored my powers because I was tired of the stress and anxiety that comes with them. But I can't just go back to my cabin, plug my ears, and hope everything works out. This is an extinction-level event unfolding here, and I intend to do what I can to stop it, even if it isn't good for my mental health."

In my peripheral vision I caught both my kids smiling, and then felt Emmaline place her hand on my shoulder and squeeze lightly.

"I'm going to go where the fight is. Wherever that man is. Wherever the best minds are working to try to solve this moon crisis. I'll go where I need to go, but I cannot run away anymore."

Everyone cheered as though I'd just delivered the Gettysburg Address. Enthusiastic clapping and yelling ensued from everyone except Bentley. Eventually we quieted and turned to hear his thoughts.

"I'm so afraid," he said softly. "I've spent so long just trying to get him back . . . how could I abandon him again to go fight in some war? Who would I leave him with? But what if the war is necessary and without fighting it we all lose?" By now tears were streaming down his face.

And then something unexpected and magical occurred. My youngest, Henry, stood from his position on the boat, walked directly to Bentley, and hugged him. Then he turned and sat next to him, and spoke.

"I don't know you very well. Don't know your son at all. Sometimes I feel like I barely even know my own family. But . . . if I were held captive by this Superintendent guy and forced to use my powers for his bidding . . . but then I got out and got rescued?"

Bentley just nodded expectantly.

"I'd wanna kick his ass," Henry revealed, much to my own delight.

"There are plenty of remote areas along the river among the Mississippi Lowland Forests." Bentley was giving us a geography lesson. "Some areas might be underwater. But there's a lot of land ahead of us where we can square off with authorities without involving innocent citizens."

Everyone sighed collectively.

"But," he continued.

Everyone stopped sighing.

"It's only one of three sites we need to choose. We also need to find three sites equally empty of citizens, each two-hundred fifty miles away in specific directions."

"What?" Freddie balked instantly.

"I don't understand," Winnie offered, backing him up.

Even Emmaline and Patrick were squinting at the images on Bentley's computer.

"Okay, let's just go through this line by line," Bentley finally said, a half-smile in his voice. I wondered how often he had to dumb down his ideas for a regular audience and concluded it was probably a lot. But he never seemed to tire of sharing his knowledge. He should have been a teacher. Maybe he still could be.

He continued. "If we use our powers along the river in some forest . . . we believe that activity will be detected by the Finder, who's extending his power's range using my son's ability. And that will mark our location and bring the heat. But it won't necessarily bring the Finder and my son here. All we know is that he'll be in a five-hundred-mile range of where we used our powers. We could start a skirmish all for nothing."

Most of us nodded, though we were all still a little confused. At least I was.

"In order to ensure that my son and the Finder end up here, at our intended location along the river . . . we have to box them in." Bentley drew on a piece of paper for a bit, before holding it up and gesturing to it as he talked. "We have to use our powers in three different places, each exactly two-hundred fifty miles from our forest location. We have to stagger using the powers, but if we do it right . . . that will naturally lead the Finder and therefore my son to our spot in the forest, because that will be the only location where they can keep tabs on all three of their tracked power users."

"What?" I stated blankly.

"It's basic triangulation," he offered, as though that alone explained everything to me.

I just stammered.

"He's right, Dad," Winnie offered.

My daughter was better at math than I was at self-doubt, which is to say she was exceptional at it. If she was concurring with Bentley's math, then I was ready to hop on board as well. "That's good enough for me."

And plans commenced.

Patrick would be sent to just northeast of Baton Rouge, roughly two-hundred fifty miles south. Freddie and his gargantuan ability would be sent to the west and a little north, to the Ozark National Forest. And finally, Winnifred was sent up to rural southwest Tennessee.

Before she left, I bumped foreheads and locked arms—my tradition for father/daughter advice, though it was usually mostly comical advice about not eating yellow snow and the like—what can I say, fathers do strange things while bonding with their kids. This time the advice was serious. "I love you and I trust you. You're going to do fine. All you need to do is use your power to get noticed, then use it to get back here lickety-split."

"I'll be fine, Dad," she blushed. "It's not the first time I've used my gift to try to get a guy's attention."

I clearly went white or something because she immediately got awkward and said, "I mean . . ." and then she turned and jogged away. "Oh my God," I heard her mutter.

"We're going to talk about this later," I yelled after her.

The problem with our plan was the natural delay it caused. Each of our three triangulating heroes had to get out two-hundred fifty miles to their destination without using their powers. We didn't have any cars left and only had a fairly lousy boat.

Patrick and Winnie could make that distance in seconds, but they'd be using their powers to do so. Hell, even Freddie at his full size could probably traverse two-hundred fifty miles in an hour or so.

But we couldn't use our powers until we were ready to set the plan in motion. This meant all three remote heroes had to travel to their spot via traditional means; it also meant the rest of us would have a good several hours to kill while they traveled.

Bentley used his access to the satellites and found us a small river resort town named Caldwell. Based on images from last night, the town had a wealth of motorbikes and small cars for rent. So, we steered in that direction with a bit of hope in the air.

We decided not to pull off to the shore tonight and kept on trekking to reach our destination. Henry, Bentley, and I took shifts steering the ship and serving as lookout.

At some point during the night, Monster left me to snuggle up with Emmaline, and I resented him for it the next morning.

That night I had my first "sweaty dream" in seventeen years. I would define "sweaty dream" for you if it weren't painfully and embarrassingly obvious.

In this dream, I was on a raft in space, with both my children. There were faceless rowers on rafts all around us, rowing as though space were water, and my kids were both newborn babies I held in each arm while still trying to row.

I looked down at my first child on the left with love, only to see a toothy bottomless hole of fear and pain. I quickly turned to look at my second child's face, and it was a blank painter's canvas. It stayed blank, despite my expectations, and I was ultimately haunted by its blank nothingness.

"I guess this is my life now," I said to myself on my space raft. "Oh, there's Saturn! Hey, it's so pretty up close!"

"Okay, so, let's make sure we're all on the same page," Bentley said quietly.

We had reached our destination along the river, trudged into the middle of a dense forest, and had set up camp and started a fire. Winnie, Freddie, and Patrick were all gone, racing toward their destinations on motorcycles on a mission to help us lure in the Finder.

I was greatly concerned about my daughter's motorcycle breaking down. Or her encountering someone or something on the journey that sought to do her harm—after all, they'd all been borrowed/stolen from local homes.

I made her promise she would use her powers to escape any creeps she felt threatened by. But that didn't make me feel any less anxious.

Anxious. There was that feeling again. Only I hadn't actually started using my powers again just yet . . . *interesting*.

Anyway, with the three remote folks gone, that left Bentley, myself, Henry, and Emmaline. And Monster, of course, as well as Pat's dog, Leroy.

"Once all our agents activate their powers in succession, it's only a matter of time before the Finder—and hopefully my son—arrive here, at this very spot. At that point, we will likely also be facing a ton of military power."

I nodded. Em nodded. My little man Henry just silently nodded same as his parents had, though I could sense his fear.

Bentley looked up at the crumbling moon, which now appeared to clearly have four large pieces, two of which were falling toward the Earth. "Looks like it's gonna be days instead of weeks on this moon situation."

In spite of my abject fear, I replied calmly. "One thing at a time. Solve one problem, then move on to the next one."

"Okay, but on that first problem, Phil," Bentley said softly, "really banking on you coming out of retirement here. We're gonna need your skills. I don't mean to be judgy, but it's been a while. Your son can do a kind of force field defense, I'm told, which is awesome, but . . . I can't do shit. It's you and Emmaline handling this battle, basically."

"I'll be fine," I said. It was said with calm and confidence and an edge of anger, and Bentley got the picture immediately.

I went to a new headspace. All my concerns and worries evaporated—my brain shoving them aside for now—and I went into battle mode. "This won't be a problem."

Emmaline, having only seen me this confident a time or two in all of history, bent down and whispered to Henry, "This is going to be epic; don't blink during this fight, kid, or you'll miss something special."

15

COME AND GET ME

The power inside me . . . I didn't trust it. I thought of it as a dragon, an uncontrollable but massive force. I hadn't just quit using my powers because of my mental health, though that was the main reason. I'd also quit because I was scared of how powerful I was becoming.

And yet . . .

What if I'm rusty? What if I can't do what I think I can do? What if all these years of not using my powers has weakened them? Or I've lost them altogether?

I think I mentioned how good I was at self-doubt, no? I was the Michael Jordan of self-doubt. I suddenly worried things might not go as planned here; that we might rescue the kid but I fail and the DHS takes me.

I turned.

"Bentley, I can't see any reason for you to be here for this. Or Henry. I want you to take him and get somewhere nearby and safe. There's a small ridge of hills a half mile away to the west; you could hide there until this all blows over."

"Phillip," he seemed hurt, "I can contribute to this. I know I can't shoot lasers, but you've seen me on the battlefield. I make a difference!"

"You definitely make a difference, which is why I'm asking you to look after my son. We'll still be in radio range; you will still have your access to the satellites. You can help me from over there just as much as you could from right here—right or wrong?"

"Right or wrong" was something we used to bark at each other during an argument back in the day to try to end it early by forcing the other guy to admit you were right about one part of the debate. I was excellent at deploying this technique.

"Dad," Henry whined. "I can help too! My power is defensive!"

"You bet your ass it is," I agreed with him. "And I need you to use it to protect you and Bentley when this all goes down."

"What about you?" he sniffed.

"Believe me, buddy," I smiled, "I can take care of myself."

"He can take care of himself," Bentley agreed as he took Henry by the shoulder and they started their hike.

I turned to Em. "It's been a long time since we've done this together."

"Longer for you than for me," she reminded, a devilish smile in her eyes. "Do you still have that harness Bentley created?"

"Ha," I laughed. "No. That's probably in a storage shed somewhere."

"Just as well," she smiled. "We're more used to being individuals than part of a team."

She didn't mean it to be hurtful. She wasn't trying to make a wry joke. She just meant that, quite literally, we didn't have any recent experience working together.

But it still stung.

"Let's just remember we're after the kid. That's all. Everything else is gravy. Once we get the kid, we're out of here."

"To that place," she replied.

"To that place, yes," I concurred. "After the mini-jump over to get Bentley and Henry, of course."

"Of course," she replied.

I hugged her, then fell to my knees, arms still around her legs.

"You have to stop apologizing, Phillip. You thought I was dead. You had to move on. I'm not mad about it."

"I'm not hugging you as an apology anymore," I choked. "I'm hugging you to make up for lost time. And because . . . soon . . . I might lose the ability to hug you again . . . depending on how this battle goes."

Two hours later, after we'd each consumed a cold can of beans, Emmaline and I decided to huddle together for warmth. We knew things would kick off soon, but it made sense to conserve body warmth until then.

All three of our remote power-users should have been in place by now, given six hours had passed since they'd departed. That allowed for stops for gas, traffic, and the two-hundred-fifty miles of travel.

According to the plan, we were moments away from things getting started.

Patrick was supposed to go first, and I assumed he was just going to run in circles like he used to do back when he was a preschooler.

Freddie would go next, ten minutes later, growing to full size and beating up some buildings for a few moments before shrinking and taking cover in a basement for just a bit.

Then it would be Winnie's turn, and while I suspected she had more in mind than merely racing around in circles, her job was to similarly distract any authorities around her while showing off her abilities for a bit.

Thanks to Bentley's hacking abilities, we were able to listen in on the dispatch channel for DHS. We thought it would provide a strategic advantage, and it did, but it ultimately provided more of a humor advantage than anything else.

"We've got power activity detected. Just outside of Baton Rouge. Looks like three seconds of power usage, sir."

"How far are we?"

"Four hundred miles, sir."

"Make course for Baton Rouge; let me know when we are inside two-hundred fifty miles."

"Will do, sir."

A few moments of crackling silence passed on the radio.

"Sir—" came a different, more urgent voice.

"Yes."

"Powers detected to the northwest. Ozarks, sir . . . reports of a giant, which lines up with our readings from the Finder, sir."

"Okay," an authoritative voice boomed. "Split all resources on the ground and in the air, half to Baton Rouge and half to the Ozarks."

"Roger that, resources splitting."

I couldn't help but smile as the DHS played right into our hand. I giggled as their trucks and helicopters repeatedly changed directions based on the latest information.

Finally, it was time for Winnie to make her move. Without direct comms, I said a quick prayer that she remembered her roots and her training and then waited to hear the DHS radio transmission.

"Boss," a nervous voice said over the DHS radio system. "You don't want to hear this, but I have a third use of powers, confirmed, in southwestern Tennessee, just outside of Memphis."

A scrambling of voices then talked over each other for a moment. One of those voices was cussing profusely. Finally, one voice took control.

"Goddammit," a voice bellowed over the DHS airwaves. "We hired that nerd for a reason. Someone wake his ass up and get him to do the math and tell me where I need to go so that all three of these spots can be monitored while we figure out how to respond! And he better pray to Holy Jesus there isn't a fourth incident."

This was going exactly according to plan, and I chided myself for being surprised, given how many successful "Bentley plans" I'd already lived through in my relatively short life.

The DHS response to our action was revealing and surprising. And informative, I suppose, if we foresaw this kind of thing happening again.

After finding the center point—our location—the actual agents of the DHS were sent out in waves, like sonar, forever scoping out its own near-future path.

It was actually a cornucopia pattern, designed to ensure that wherever the answers lay they'd eventually be scooped up and discovered.

I admired it, but only briefly.

The DHS radio chirped. "Alright, sir, the triangulation point seems to be along the Mississippi River. Transmitting coordinates now."

We stayed hidden. We knew they would send some troops with the Finder and Graham Crittendon, but we also expected that those forces would be light. And while a fight was probably inevitable, grabbing the kid and clearing him from the scene was the first priority. We reminded ourselves that they didn't think any custodians were here. They just thought this was a central location to keep tracking custodial behavior elsewhere.

"Wanderers have returned home," Bentley said into our earpieces. This meant that Winnie, Patty, and Freddie had all returned to our general location and rejoined Bent and Henry up on the ridge—Patrick and Winnie had both zapped over to the Ozarks to grab Freddie and make his return nearly as instant as theirs.

"Excellent," I radioed back. "Everyone stay put until Em has the kid. She will then join you and you'll all take off together to a safe place. I'll follow after the fight is over."

"I don't like all the secrecy," Bentley admitted.

"It's not a secret. You will be with your son the whole time. We just don't want to say the location over radio in case anyone is listening or any amateur somehow hears and records this conversation. For now, only Emmaline and I know the location."

"Alright," he agreed, even though he didn't have much choice.

"Let's go radio silent for now," I added.

My stomach rumbled.

"Are you hungry?" Em asked with a smile.

"Not sure. Hungry or sick. I don't often know the difference anymore."

"Well, I've got some trail mix if you need to eat."

"There's no time. Besides, I'm legitimately not sure if it would help or hurt."

"I guess I never realized exactly how much the anxiety impacted you physically," she admitted.

"Yeah," I laughed. "It's not fun."

"I've got air and ground vehicles approaching from the northeast and the southeast. Over." It was Bentley, certainly just trying to make sure we woke up out of our mental health discussion in time to do some battle.

16

SHOW OF FORCE

The Finder and Graham Crittendon were both soft-landed fifty yards from us on the river's edge by what appeared to be a flyer—a custodian with the power of flight.

The dragon within me growled.

Shortly after they touched down, a dozen more personnel landed via parachutes. But these were researchers and scientists, from the looks of things.

However, three of them branched off and started building more of a command center–type tent, complete with radio gear and excessive maps.

It was honestly eerie watching our plan happening before my very eyes.

I turned to Em and signed, "*You need to be ready to move. As soon as you see Graham alone, you grab him and take him to the ridge. Even if you see him alone but touching one other person—especially in that case—because that person is likely the Finder and we want to also rescue that person from the Superintendent's control as well!*"

Em just smiled, kissed me, and gave me two thumbs up to indicate she understood.

I had the benefit of bionic eyes, complete with night vision and fifty times zoom capabilities. I could tell if the screws a mile away were Phillips or flathead. I tried not to flex about it much, since there were real custodians born with enhanced vision, and I didn't want to rain on their whole thing.

Anyway, I had a great view of the Amplifier and the Finder together on the beach. They did arrive with plenty of armed escorts in close quarters, but it was hard to tell, at first, if any of the guards were physically touching the "prisoners." This was an important thing to know, given our escape plan for these folks.

Although, eh . . . maybe even if a guard is touching them, we zap them out and let the heroes on the ridge take out the sudden guard? I wondered to myself.

Eventually the patterns of the folks on the beach shifted just enough to show that Graham and the Finder were separated from the group of soldiers near them.

"Ridge, can you confirm the DHS members are not touching the kid or the Finder?" I barked over the radio.

"Affirmative," Bentley replied. "Ten feet or more away."

"Is Graham touching the Finder?"

"Not at present," he said, remaining quite professional throughout this entire exchange, which was a nice surprise after our recent argument, if I do say so myself. "Very close, though."

"Man, I'd love to grab that Finder too," I said aloud, mostly to myself. "But I don't want to wait. Em, go get the kid," I declared.

Ooph!

"Bent," I whispered into the radio, "I need satellite help here to make sure I can whale on the bad guys without hurting the Finder, who I think is pretty innocent in all this."

"I, uh," the voice was Emmaline's. "I grabbed them both. They were two feet apart, so I put a hand on each of them and jumped."

"Outstanding!" I responded.

"I thought for sure you were going to be mad."

"Ha ha ha," I laughed into the radio. "I'm going to be mad, alright, but not at you. You did a good thing. Now I can focus all my anger on these DHS fools sure to descend on the spot where their bread-and-butter just disappeared from. Now you get everyone up there to the place, ASAP!"

"Copy," she replied. "Love you."

"Love you too."

I couldn't hear them poof away, but I was sure they were gone. Some, like the kids, would want to linger and watch my battle, but I knew she was too disciplined for that.

I knew I was still hidden, roughly fifty yards from the tents that had been set up, which I could only assume were a sort of base camp for operations. There were large dunes and even some rock formations along the river, and I was able to peek around and watch them without them noticing me.

I was waiting for more troops to arrive. So far there seemed to be about two dozen personnel, but most appeared to be setting up equipment or using the equipment. Only a handful were armed. But they were all in panic mode now that the Finder and Amplifier were suddenly missing.

More troops would arrive in mere seconds, and I was waiting so that I could do as much damage as possible.

This is a mistake, I told myself. *I'm going to flame out and then be killed in a hail of bullets. Who takes seventeen years off and then thinks they can perform at peak level? An idiot, that's who.*

I zoomed my bionic eyes in on the main tent to better inspect the gear. It was mostly communications stuff, like an operations trailer for a football game broadcast. Receivers, monitors, computers, equalizers, headphones. It definitely wasn't a science tent. They weren't here to study.

Suddenly an aircraft appeared overhead, lowering itself rapidly. It was one of the DHS's new transport ships, privately commissioned by Roening Corp, that were capable of maneuvering like a jet or a helicopter—like a Harrier, only bigger. As it hovered ten feet off the beach, dozens of troops jumped off and ran to file up.

Is that all? That can't be it. Their biggest weapon was just taken out from under them. They're sending more than thirty soldiers, right?

As though they were listening to me, just then, two huge submarines rose to the surface of the river, each dumping hundreds more troops onto the beach via rafts.

Should I strike now? That's a lot of firepower. Submarines! I think I'm gonna—

Just then a smaller aircraft landed, a standard helicopter. But it was carrying a very nonstandard payload.

I watched in shock as the Superintendent himself descended the stairs of the chopper and walked toward the main communications tent.

And something inside me took over. Something . . . feral. I'd never felt anything quite like this.

In movies I'd often seen vampires portrayed as needing blood in a compulsory sort of way—as much as it was food for them, they were still being drawn by a force stronger than their own will.

I felt the same.

That man was the devil, as far as I was concerned. And here I was, fifty yards away, completely unbeknownst to him.

I could end this man.

Better yet, I could apprehend this man, so he could eventually be held accountable for all the shit he pulled while in office.

Why am I even here? Why did I stay behind? I wanted violence, right? Is that bad? What does it say about me that it takes no time after the idea of using my powers again for me to be wanting to use them on a massive scale?

Maybe I should just leave.

Why don't I ever know what to do? I kicked at the massive rock that served as my shelter, but a few pieces came loose, clapping together as they fell to the ground.

Oh no!

I turned. Sure enough, every single member of the DHS camp was looking in my direction. *Oh well, no option now but to fight,* I told myself, as though I couldn't have just flown away.

In hindsight, I'd just suppressed my powers for so long . . . and maybe I'd forgotten or failed to recognize that some part of me had enjoyed using my powers, even despite the anxiety it brought on.

Whatever.

I jumped the rock and aimed my arms, palms open, and set about trying to knock them all back a few paces . . . help them realize I didn't need to be up close and hand-to-hand to kick their asses. My arms lunged into the darkness . . .

But nothing happened.

I looked down at my arms, then back up at the soldiers, who were now moving toward me, guns drawn.

Once again I pushed my arms forward, hands out, and once again nothing happened.

"Put your hands up!" I heard one of them yell.

I closed my eyes and practiced a breathing exercise I'd used all my life. I knew the soldiers were inching closer, but you can't rush a breathing exercise, at least not if you want it to be effective.

Twenty seconds later I opened my eyes. The men were probably twenty feet away. There were only a dozen of them coming at me.

One more try, I told myself.

Arms up again, palms out, concentrating with all my might and . . . nothing happened.

"This is embarrassing," I said, mostly to myself.

Some of the soldiers started to laugh. I couldn't blame them. I bet I looked ridiculous.

"Are you a custodian?" one of them mocked.

"Yeah," said another, "what's your power, dance karate?"

A third chimed in, saying, "Maybe his powers stopped working now that the moon exploded." It was clear he was being sarcastic, which suggested that even DHS troops knew how insane the Superintendent was.

They all chuckled.

I wasn't sure how to play this scenario. My powers weren't working. I had no backup.

I flirted with the idea of continuing to "act" the part of a crazy person who believed he was a custodian when he was, in fact, not. But I was never a very good actor. But also . . . I wouldn't be acting.

I still had fifteen feet or so before they were upon me. I stretched out my arms, palms out, and repeatedly tried to will my powers back to life so I could knock these guys down.

More laughter.

"Why," I tried again. "Won't," and again. "You," I wound up for one last try, "WORK!"

A short but strong burst of force flowed through my arms and hands, shot out directly in front of me, smacked the lead soldier in the abdomen, and sent him flying sixty yards away beyond the tents with a pitiful yelp that faded immediately.

"Oh!" I cried in joy at the return of my powers, followed by another "Oh!" in sudden realization of what I'd just done to that man.

Instantaneously, I was struck by four or five sharp projectiles in my arms and my neck. "Oh," I sighed as I fell to the side.

I was out before I hit the ground.

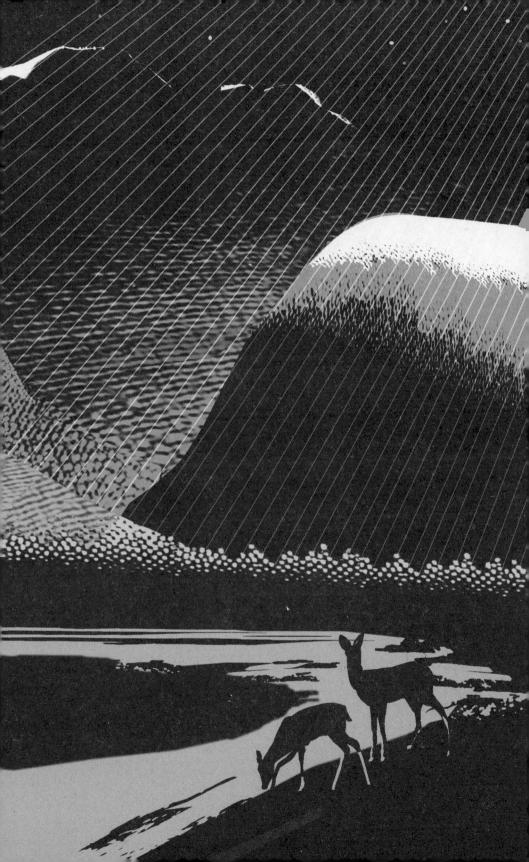

17

X HOURS LATER

I awoke in the same spot, sometime later. Face in the dirt, body contorted in an unnatural way.

What the hell?

I was confused and groggy, like a bad hangover only worse. I hadn't had too many hangovers, but I'd experienced enough to know they suck.

Where are the soldiers?

I lifted my head and saw no sign of the former DHS camp along the riverbank. My head returned quickly to the ground.

Ow. Why am I so weak?

I lifted my arm slowly to rub my forehead. I needed a pain reliever badly but I was woefully short on supplies. I moved on to massage my sore neck and brushed past two small bumps that were tender to the touch.

Oh yeah, they drugged me.

Slowly and with a great deal of difficulty, I pushed myself up into a sitting position and glanced around the immediate area.

There was the large rock I'd been hiding behind. There was the small bunch of stones I had kicked free. But no soldiers. No tents. No radios.

They even took back the tranquilizer darts they'd used to subdue me—I suddenly remembered the darts that had hit my arms, and felt around for those bumps as well. I found them, as well as a large needle mark in my left arm.

Hmm. IV? How long was I out?

The DHS had long possessed rapid DNA testing capabilities, and those only required a drop, a simple finger prick. They wouldn't have drawn blood from my arm to do a DNA test— *Oh no! They know who I am!*

I touched my right thumb and forefinger together and, sure enough, there was light pain. It had been years since I'd had a finger prick for any kind of blood test, but I knew from experience that I bruised easily on my extremities.

This was bad news.

Until now, I was not known to them. I mean . . . I was known to them, in that they had my DNA on file, and that it was connected to Em's and Dad's, and that they knew I was a powerful custodian who had gone off the grid years ago. They might have even studied me at whatever their version of police academy looked like, since I'd ended up entangled in so many of the so-called famous custodian events in modern history.

But they didn't know I was actively back in the game. They didn't know I had come out of my cave. They had no idea I was involved in the plot to find and rescue Graham Crittendon. At least . . . they hadn't until now.

Now they had evidence that one of the most powerful custodians ever was out and about using his powers again and they did . . . nothing? They just let me go? I don't want to be cocky, but I felt like my reputation should have rung a few more bells.

This doesn't make any sense.

I finally got the courage to stand to my feet, though I needed the large rock to steady myself or else I would have slid back to the dirt quickly.

How long was I out?

It was evening when we had first arrived, and well into night when all the action went down. But now the sun was up—though it was still early, judging by its position in the sky.

I was glad to see the sun and to feel its warmth washing over me. Over on the other side of the world, while we were getting the sun's glad tidings, they were getting the harrowing view of the broken and falling moon.

I for one was glad not to have to look at it for a while.

Why didn't they kill me? Even if I had no value as a prisoner, which itself is strange, surely, they would have killed me, since I'm a custodian and they hate custodians . . . right? They either turn or kill custodians, but me they left here next to a river?

Something was off, but there wasn't enough information for me to figure it out. It didn't help that I was still feeling sluggish in body and brain. I tried to stand without the help of the rock, and was surprised to succeed . . . momentarily.

Alright, Em would have taken everyone up to the old abandoned base in the far northwest from our adventures from years past. We weren't trying to give Bentley any kind of PTSD or flashback to his villain days, it was just a fairly safe place we all knew that was so far out of the way that the DHS was unlikely to look for us out there.

But I was supposed to arrive there within an hour. They would have been expecting me long before that, but by the time an hour passed, they should have gotten worried.

I looked at the sky again.

It's definitely been more than an hour.

So something was keeping her from checking on me. That was an ominous realization, but I shoved it aside for now.

Why did they let me go?

I couldn't get over it. Maybe it was my ego getting in the way. Maybe I was offended because I saw myself as more of a "prize prisoner" for custodian haters than I truly was? Did they see me as old and washed up? Had my sorry display of rusty powers caused them more than a fit of laughter?

I kept putting myself in my enemy's mindset and I couldn't find a single good reason to let me go. There just didn't seem to be any logic to it whatsoever. They could have even maybe tried bargaining my release for the Finder or Graham. It wouldn't have worked, but you'd think they'd have tried it. Instead . . . nothing.

A new terrible idea emerged: What if they found something wrong with me when they tested my blood? Something that told them I was going to die soon anyway? Like cancer or something? So, I became useless to them. Like when the aliens in movies pass by some random human and we find out later it's because they smelled diseases on them and such? I couldn't remember the last time I had been to the doctor. Was I sick?

And then I figured, maybe they were watching me right now to see what I would do or where I would go. Maybe they hoped I'd lead them to the rest of the group. I looked up again, maxed out my zoom on the magic eyeballs, and saw nothing resembling a satellite or drone overhead, which didn't mean they weren't there, of course.

I sighed loudly.

I need more information, I thought again. *A lot more. Maybe I should investigate the area where their camp was set up. I might find some kind of clue they left behind.*

Before I could go any further, I heard a familiar and welcome sound.

Ooph!

"Em! Where the hell have you been?" I shouted in a mix of joy and frustration.

"It's a long story," she replied.

"Dad!" the kids yelled as they grabbed me around the waist.

Freddie and Bentley talked over each other as they greeted me, so the most I could make out was, "We're glad you thought aren't dead." I got the gist of it, I think.

"Phillip, I'd like you to meet my son, Graham, and our new friend Edmund."

"Hello, Graham, it's nice to finally meet you."

"You too, sir." He seemed starstruck.

"Edmund," I said, shaking the young man's hand. "Nice to make your acquaintance."

Monster happy-whined and marched up to greet me. "Monster, I missed you, buddy!" He hugged me as usual, but then he got distracted sniffing my chest, and then he stepped back a few feet and lightly growled. "Monster?"

"That's weird," Winnie added. "He loves Daddy more than anyone."

"Well, he's been through a lot lately," I offered. "He isn't used to teleporting, that's for sure."

"That's true," Winnie agreed.

"My first teleport made me throw up," Freddie offered.

"Buddy?" I tried again.

"Odd," Em agreed.

"Maybe he smells the tranquilizer chemicals in my bloodstream?" I offered. I'd heard stories of dogs smelling cancer and other diseases in clinical trials. It didn't seem too far-fetched an idea, especially in a world with super-heroes.

"They tranqued, you, eh?" It was Bentley. "I was wondering why there wasn't a crater in the ground here by now."

"Yeah, about that, though," I replied, pausing to build up my self-esteem a bit before continuing. "I actually couldn't use my powers at first. I kept trying over and over and nothing happened. Like, nothing at all. I looked like an idiot thrashing my arms around with nothing to show for it. Those soldiers were even laughing at me like I was a lunatic. Finally, eventually, something clicked and the powers came back to life and I sent . . . some poor bastard flying way further than I intended. Then they tranqued me. I woke up here a few minutes ago."

Monster wasn't growling anymore but he was still wary and keeping a small distance between us.

"Well, if that's it, that'll eventually wear off," Bentley added hopefully before getting back to business. "You don't remember anything?"

"Remember?" I asked. "I don't remember a thing, no." I lifted my right hand. "They took my blood, obviously." I then lifted my left arm. "They also put a needle here, God knows what for."

"That's terrifying," Freddie exclaimed.

"They weren't just drawing blood?" Em asked.

"They pricked my finger here, and that's basically only for a single drop of blood. They can test my DNA from a single drop."

"Right," she agreed, "but maybe they drew more from your arm for other reasons."

I paused for a moment. It was a new and interesting thought that hadn't occurred to me.

But Bentley had the answer.

"If they were going to draw a vial from his arm for some kind of testing or other nefarious purpose, they'd have just included the DNA test in that run. They wouldn't take blood from two places."

"So then what's the needle mark for?" Emmaline asked, rather concerned.

"They must've put something in," Bentley replied.

A few hours later we had our plan.

Everyone knew their part. We had talked it through several times while feasting on more fresh fish from the mighty Mississippi.

There were two missions now: keeping Graham and the Finder safe from the Superintendent's henchmen at the DHS, and trying to find a way to stop the moon crisis. Both were unspeakably difficult tasks, but despite that, optimism was high.

As much as we all loved Bentley's kid, everyone agreed that the planet's safety was the more important of the two missions—yes, even Bentley. Heck, even Graham himself agreed. The Earth and the remainder of humanity was more important than any of us, or even the entire group of us.

But still . . . keeping the kid safe was also super freaking important, because the enemy could grow much stronger in a short period of time if he somehow grabbed the kid again and regained control of that ability.

So it was decided that everyone but myself would be devoted to the moon crisis. I was considered the "strongest" of the lot of us, and we needed to maximize firepower while minimizing manpower when it came to protecting these kids. That was me in a nutshell.

Bentley's mind was also crucial to finding a scientific solution for things, such as the moon dilemma. Em's ability could be invaluable in terms of procuring supplies or new helpers. Freddie's raw strength was never a detriment. Even my kids' abilities could assist in the moon plan.

Of course, any plan to save the moon was kind of counting on Graham's amplifying ability to factor in, because that would make everyone involved ten times more powerful. We were banking on it—which only made my job protecting him all the more critical.

So the plan was for me to keep him safe and hidden—along with the Finder—until we were needed at the very end of the moon plan.

God help us all.

18

PREVIOUSLY ON . . . THE FINDER

The Finder was not what any of us expected.

As soon as the group landed up at the old abandoned base, a collective cheer went up except for one person: the Finder.

Instead of cheering, he was shouting.

"What have you done? Do you know? Do you even know? I work for the Superintendent!"

As the group quieted down and listened, Emmaline and Bentley engaged the man.

"We know," Bentley said. "We've freed you from his control."

"We're trying to help you," Em added.

"Well, thanks a lot," the young man spat. "Now my family is going to die!"

He appeared to be in his late teens or early twenties.

"Oh no!" Em said. "What did I do?" She worried there had been more innocent people at that campsite that she'd missed and failed to save.

"I work for that vile man only because he has my mother and my two sisters under surveillance, with henchmen ready to kill them the moment I stop obeying him. I'm unique, you see," he breathed rapidly, "I can tell when people use their powers."

"We know, that's why we rescued you," Freddie said, not really helping in the moment.

"He didn't give me a choice. I mean . . . I turned him down. I even told him to kill me, and that I would never use my ability for him. But he just threatened to kill them instead." He hung his head. It was clear the stress of the situation was weighing heavily on him. "And now they're going to die because I'm not there anymore." He burst into tears.

Emmaline hugged him long and warmly.

"I don't understand," Freddie said, "we essentially kidnapped you from him . . . he can't blame you for that, can he?"

"Can I ask your name, sir?"

"Freddie."

"Freddie, if it were your mother and sisters . . . would you take the chance?"

"No," Freddie admitted.

"What's your name?" Patrick asked, trying to bring some calm to the proceedings momentarily.

"Edmund. Edmund Ramirez."

"Edmund, I'm Patrick, and I think you know Graham. This is his dad, Bentley, then Freddie, then Emmaline, and that furry guy is Monster."

"We don't have time for this," Em cut in before pointing a finger at Edmund's chest. "If what you're saying is true, then we need to act immediately to make sure no harm comes to your family. And then you're gonna help us fix the moon, you hear me?"

"Yes, ma'am."

"Now where is your mother?"

"Boston. She's in Boston." He rattled off an address.

"We're gonna go get her and your sisters."

"Thank you!" he cried.

"Patrick, you're with me. Everyone else . . . hang here . . . Phillip should be here any minute. Just fill him in and I should be back soon."

Emmaline and Patrick made short work of the stealthy evacuation of Edmund's family.

Emmaline simply popped into their living room, said something along the lines of "Edmund sent me and we're here to rescue you," and poofed back out.

There had been henchmen outside the apartment complex, and they had been on their way from the car to the building, probably to execute Edmund's family as ordered by their boss. But Patrick had messed with them—opening their car doors, flashing the lights, whooshing by them whispering things—just long enough to buy time for a clean evacuation.

The trouble had come after the rescue.

You see, Emmaline and Patrick had agreed upon a meeting spot three blocks away, in an alley. So Emmaline jumped there with Mrs. Ramirez and her daughters, and Patrick ran there lightning fast after stalling the henchmen.

Neither of them could have known that a cop's family lived above the alley, or that the cop's youngest child loved to look out the window at night instead of going to sleep like a good boy. Neither of them could have predicted that the boy would have seen both Emmaline and her stowaways appear out of thin air below, as well as Patrick's seemingly similar out-of-nowhere appearance. They couldn't know he'd run screaming into his father's room, or that the father would call his precinct, or that the captain would send the farm—local police that helped in the capture of custodians were often given cash bonuses by DHS or even offered jobs.

Every local police captain dreamt of apprehending an honest-to-goodness custodian and making the jump to the big leagues of crime fighting . . . the DHS.

So when Emmaline and Patrick turned, guests in tow, to walk calmly down the street for a few minutes to catch their breaths, they couldn't have known they were about to be surrounded by dozens of cops.

To be certain, neither Em nor Patrick panicked when they rounded the corner and saw all the cops. This was not a situation they couldn't handle quickly and easily. It was more of a minor inconvenience than a true hurdle.

Emmaline merely put her hand out and asked everyone to put their hands in. Once everyone was touching someone that was touching Em's hand . . . she just teleported out of there instantly, leaving the cops scratching their butts.

The problem was where she jumped to.

None of the Ables crew had been back to Freepoint in five years or more at least. The hero cities were among the first places the Superintendent's DHS troops attacked back when he declared war on custodians.

There was nothing to go back for, ultimately. In fact, the entire town had been razed. All that remained were basements and rubble. A few walls still stood, but only partially, and nothing anyone could recognize.

The high school? Gone. Jack's Pizza? Flattened. My old house? Buried under debris. The entire city had been obliterated.

We knew this because Patrick had gone back once, years ago. The experience had scarred him. We did not know what he had seen, but he had discouraged any other custodians from returning home after his trip.

What we did not know was that DHS had since built a giant detention and processing facility on the very site of what used to be Freepoint. Much like the old distribution centers during the heyday of commerce and capitalism, the DHS simplified its incarceration process by building and utilizing regional processing facilities.

Basically they were gigantic prisons that were used to house suspected individuals "temporarily"—which often meant months or even years, though it varied wildly from inmate to inmate—before they were finally sent on to their more permanent prison home or, in extremely rare cases, before they were eventually released.

And look, no one hates a cheap coincidence in an adventure story more than I do, because it always feels . . . cheap . . . and coincidental. But the fact remains that coincidence is a perfectly valid mathematical outcome in this universe.

So although the DHS prison built on the ashes of Freepoint—which was also directly over Emmaline's old childhood home—may have felt personal to Emmaline or anyone in her family who had lived here, the fact of the matter was, the facility had been built on a location based on access to water and electricity from existing lines already run.

Anyway, you might just now be remembering that Emmaline's reflex teleportation location in times of extreme stress or pressure is her childhood bedroom. This previously led to a very humorous and embarrassing first meeting between her father and me back in the day.

Well . . . this time, the reflex teleportation had led to Em, Patrick, and all three Ramirezes jumping directly into a holding cell of a DHS regional processing center.

The crew at the abandoned base waited around for another hour before realizing something had gone wrong on Emmaline and Patrick's mission.

At first, they began to slowly panic. But Bentley provided some solid wisdom and took the lead in comforting the troops.

"Things happen. There are variables. But I'm confident in Phillip's powers. I'm confident in Emmaline's and Patrick's powers. If it's taking longer for them to return, it's for a good reason."

After a while, that sort of talk began to ring hollow even to the one speaking it.

Bentley began to make contingency plans in case we never came back. Where would he go? How would he get there? Why would he be going there?

He looked around. He had Freddie, who had tons of experience and a helpful physical power. He had Graham, who had a power that made anyone else's power ten times stronger . . . this was also helpful. Winnifred was a speedster that even Patrick seemed in awe of, and Henry was known to make defensive force fields to protect those inside from danger.

Monster didn't have any powers, but his loyalty nearly made up for it.

It didn't take Bentley long to figure out that Patrick and Emmaline had likely been captured, and that it was up to him to save them. So he turned to his greatest strength: technology.

Actually, he'd already made the hack into DHS radio systems earlier, so all he needed to do was reestablish that connection. If his friends had been captured, he would hear about it on this radio. Eventually.

The problem was that DHS was such a massive operation, they had more than a hundred radio channels for their dispatch and communication operations.

Bentley gave everyone their own radio and their own headphones, along with their own unique DHS signal to keep track of.

An hour later Freddie heard a call from the aptly named Freepoint Holding Complex that rattled off some familiar names that were apparently soon to be transferred from holding to general population: Emmaline Sallinger, Patrick Sallinger, Rosaline Ramirez, Maria Ramirez, and Anita Ramirez.

"I don't like this," Patrick fumed.

Emmaline just laughed. "Do you think the rest of us enjoy this?"

"It's not just being imprisoned. I don't understand why we can't use our powers." He tried again to run fast and could not.

"There's only one explanation," Em replied. "This Superintendent person has found another No Power Zone custodian and he's using them to guard all the heroes he's locked up. Hell, maybe he found more than one."

"I thought NPZ heroes were extinct," Pat countered.

"Wouldn't be the first time a species believed extinct suddenly came back from the dead," Mrs. Ramirez replied.

"Well, what are we going to do now?" Patrick asked emphatically.

"There is nothing we can do," Freddie responded.

"I think now," Em replied, "we wait."

Bentley had not only learned where his friends were being held, he'd learned every single thing about that facility, from blueprint to daily warden's log. The depth and capabilities of his brain would never cease to amaze me.

He even found a hidden server that told him about the NPZ custodian who was blocking powers inside the entire facility. This NPZ user's name was Sven, and he had been genetically tinkered with at conception by scientists using his parents' DNA.

Bentley decided to hack the complex and force a fire drill.

A fire drill in this facility put a temporary hold on the general security software, to allow for all the doors to open at once and let all the prisoners and security personnel flee the fire as fast as possible.

In the event of a fire drill, even an NPZ user blocking powers in the facility would stand down and head to safety. As many DHS guards and employees were former custodians—power users—the fire regulations were intended to help those people get out safely as fast as possible.

It wouldn't last long. The prison surely had pretty good computer people on their end who would realize the fire drill had been remotely triggered. And they'd disable it and revert things quickly. But by then many prisoners would be out of their cells. It would be pandemonium.

Eventually a radio call to Sven would have him returning to his post and reengaging his ability. But if Emmaline acted quickly enough . . . if she recognized what was happening and moved immediately . . . she could get them all out.

And that's exactly what happened.

Soon, they were all back up at the abandoned base in the northwest, hugging and enjoying the reunion for a moment.

"Wait," Emmaline finally said aloud. "Phillip isn't here. Something must have gone wrong!"

19

THE MOON PLAN

Unbeknownst to most, the Superintendent had a second super-missile.

Built as a redundancy in case the first missile's attempt had failed to explode the moon satisfactorily, the rumored second missile was now considered by some in the underground custodians' movement to be the last and best chance to protect the Earth from the moon's two larger projectile parts, which were currently falling and threatening to impact the planet.

Some thought the second missile was a bit of fiction. An old wives' tale.

But if it were real . . . and if it were aimed properly, and exploded at the correct time, it was theorized that the two largest moon chunks would be blown sideways and split up into smaller parts just enough that they would glance off our atmosphere back into space rather than breaking through and destroying us all.

The Ables, such as we were these days, were great proponents of this plan. In fact, we intended to make it a reality.

Because we currently had the Finder in our possession—or more importantly, he was no longer in the possession of our enemy—we were free to use our superpowers to hop around the country and do other miracles. At least, we were free to do so without fear of instantly being found. The DHS still had a bunch of satellites, and with a bit of delay those things could probably convey some information about us to the ones chasing us.

It was a strange new world. Almost none of our moves were truly anonymous.

When was the last time they had been?

We'd found a modest fishing boat tied to a pier a few miles down the shore. It had a working motor, plenty of gas, and plenty of fishing gear.

We left a note.

Bentley had sent us on our way while gifting us with a truly incredible piece of technology he had invented, his invisible-vehicle box. This device was actually a lot simpler than it sounds. A series of small panels on top of a car—or, in this instance, a boat—projected a display above the vehicle's roof. That display consisted of the views of a system of cameras positioned around the vehicle's edges and pointed down.

So, a car's cameras would take video of the road, and send it up to the display atop the vehicle. Anyone or anything above the vehicle would see only the road when looking down. It was like a content-aware Photoshop tool, only much more sophisticated.

It worked for boats on water as well, and even planes or trains. It was genius, but Bentley was quick to insist that it wasn't his invention or technology. He'd borrowed from the experiments of others who had gone before him in this space, but I still felt like his brain had done something here the others hadn't yet accomplished.

I didn't care. It gave Graham and Edmund and me the perfect cover as we continued down the river toward New Orleans.

The plan, such as it was, was to drive this fishing boat straight through the mouth of the Mississippi River and then directly into the Gulf of Mexico before veering straight southeast toward Central Florida.

I was still considering switching boats in New Orleans, but switching boats would mean that I'd have to dismantle and reconfigure Bentley's invisibility box onto the new boat—which would be a pain in the ass and slow us down considerably.

Anyway, I had hours to make that decision. For now, the two kids were hanging out in the back of the boat. I could hear that they were talking, but I couldn't make it out.

They'd both been through a lot together as prisoners and subjects of the Superintendent. They'd probably even formed a friendship of sorts . . . a bond I could not hope to understand or ever share. But again, I was mostly concerned with our progress. Both these kids were going to need therapy, but for now, I just needed to keep them fed and alive.

The rest of the gang had to leave the river behind and hit the road again, as they were headed for Houston.

You see, NASA fires off most of their rockets from Florida—Cape Canaveral, to be specific—but their headquarters is located in Houston. Hence the whole "Houston, we have a problem" thing. They were launched from Florida, but mission control was always Houston.

So, we were going after this alternate moon missile on two different fronts: physical and software-based.

Unfortunately, there is no river from the Arkansas area straight to Houston. So the gang stole a church van. An honest-to-God—no pun intended—church van. It was an extra-long white van with four bar seats and two front bucket seats. The side had a bunch of letters scraped off, so it read "Chu of ation." I presumed it originally read "Church of the Salvation," but I might never know for certain. That was an educated guess.

Bentley only had the one invisibility machine, and he'd given it to us on the boat, so they were driving without any means of hiding their vehicle. This made them susceptible to being discovered or tracked by drones or satellites, or even pulled over by police.

But they didn't have a choice.

The roads were light on volume, so the gang just tried their best to keep the speed limit and blend in with the rest of the traffic as much as they could.

"Maybe we should sing a song?" Bentley offered.

"What kind of song?" Winnie asked, somewhat curious—she was known to sing or hum around the house and orchard.

"How about . . ." Bentley searched for a song, realizing he wasn't much of a singer himself. "How about ninety-nine bottles of beer?"

Emmaline shot him a dirty look.

"What? It's not like they don't know that beer exists," he countered.

"What's it about?" Henry asked.

"Well, it's a repeating song. So you sing about all the bottles on the wall. It goes like this:

Ninety-nine bottles of beer on the wall
Ninety-nine bottles of beer
You take one down, pass it around
Ninety-eight bottles of beer on the wall.

"Then you repeat it, but with ninety-eight and ninety-seven . . . and you keep going until you reach zero."

There was a long pause before Winnie spoke frankly. "That is the dumbest song I've ever heard of. You want me to sing the same stupid short melody over and over again a hundred times?"

"Technically," Bent corrected her, "only ninety-nine times."

Winnie screamed and moved to the rear seat, lying down so they couldn't see her.

"What?" Bentley asked.

The broken pieces of the moon were getting closer, growing larger. It was uncomfortable to look at, at least if you were used to standard moon-watching. Actually, even if you rarely looked up at the moon, I'd imagine this cracked and falling version would still be unsettling.

I decided to get my mind off such serious things with a good old-fashioned distraction, if only for my own well-being.

"There's no reason we can't get to know each other," I said, stepping away from the wheel long enough to bound up two steps and talk to my teenage shipmates. "Come on down here into the cabin. Let's make something to eat."

Ten minutes later—thank God for microwaves—we were all eating miniature raviolis and drinking warm diet soda.

"Alright, I'll start," I said as they continued to finish their meals. "I grew up with your dad, Graham. You probably knew that already. We were the best of friends all through middle school and high school and even into college."

"Until he turned evil," Graham said rather bluntly.

I was taken aback. "Well, I don't know that I think he ever turned evil, but he had some pain, and in the midst of that pain he decided to act against his better judgment." I was extremely proud of my careful wording.

"He turned evil," Graham reiterated casually. "He's sorry. He told me all about it. It's cool, but he did turn evil."

"If you say so," I replied. "Regardless . . . the point is that he's good now, and he's going to help us save the world."

"You ever think about the consequences of having children?" Graham suddenly and shockingly barked. "Ever?"

I looked at him for a moment before responding to the odd query. "Well, I'm not sure what you mean," I replied earnestly.

"You were born blind, right?"

"I was."

"So, you had a chance that your own kid would be born blind, right? Genetically speaking?" His anger was palpable and it scared me, though I was still determined to root out the cause of his anger to offer a salve.

"Yes, I suppose so."

"So knowing all that . . . despite that freaking risk . . . you still had a kid? I mean . . . just how do you justify that?" He was apoplectic. He simply didn't understand any point of view besides his own—but he was coming from a place of anger.

And I reminded myself he was still very young, as well as in the midst of a crisis that would frighten almost anyone in his position.

"I guess I don't believe that a disability makes someone less human," I offered. I shrugged in an exaggerated fashion. I was trying to avoid a fight, not exacerbate one. But I wasn't sure how much control I had over that.

"Whatever," he replied.

I hadn't been prepared for young Graham to have so much vitriol.

"My dad has trouble walking," he suddenly continued, shaking me out of my own thoughts. "Mom has skin issues with the weather. But they still thought, 'Hey, let's the two of us frail people create a new life that may or may not end up with one or both of our afflictions.'"

I smiled as honestly as possible. "You can keep going if you want, Graham. I have my own beefs with your dad, not to mention how many complaints I have about my own father. This is a safe place to vent, my man."

"I don't want to vent," he screamed. "I want to go back in time and have a father who's there. And I don't want any stupid powers. I just want a dad!"

"You can't do it," I said, calmly but directly. "Can't go back, kid. So now how do you want to deal with those emotions? You wanna bottle them up forever? Or do you want to address them head on and ultimately move beyond them?"

I wished my old therapist could see me now, putting a kid's mental health ahead of everything else.

"What do you know?" Graham shot back, before climbing back out onto the bow.

"I know that I used to wish I'd never been born. For many of the same reasons you mention," I said quietly. "I know what it's like to have a father so devoted to hero work you rarely see him. I know what it's like to be kidnapped, imprisoned, and forced to use my powers for evil against my will. I even know how much it hurts to use my own powers to rip pain-chips out of my own hand! So I think I know enough to know, you know?!"

Graham was quiet. He nodded. "You're right. I don't know as much as you know."

"It's not about how much I know, Graham, it's about your life. You have X amount of years to live. That's it. At some point you're going to die. Your father will also die, which means you have X-minus-Y number of years alive that you can spend with him. The past is the past. Your father is sorry and has told you so, and will continue to tell you so. But those years are gone, buddy. They're gone forever. You cannot go back in time and get a second childhood. All you can do is try to maximize the years you have left together and make those golden. You have Z number of years left together; do you want to spend them bitching about the past or do you want to enjoy them? Because anger, at least long-term anger, is a choice."

20

TEXAS

It was safe to say that none of the Ables in the church van headed for Houston had ever set foot in Texas. At the first in-state stop for refreshments, cowboy hats were on nearly everyone's purchase agenda, as though everyone had momentarily forgotten what kind of trip they were really on.

And who could blame them for needing a little time to blow off steam?

"Oh my . . . um . . . stop in Texas and buy a cowboy hat . . . how original! You know, wearing one of those does not make you—" Bentley was bumped mid-sentence by another cowboy-hat-wearing patron. "Fine," he said, giving in to the universe. "Waste your money on truck stop tokens and trinkets. See if I care."

"Bentley," Emmaline said softly, "let them enjoy themselves. If we're right about Houston, these kids are all going to have to focus on serious things very soon. Let's let them have some fun. What do you say?"

"Fine," Bentley said, waving his hand over his head before then working his way back out of the store and into the van. "You know we *do* have an agenda," he muttered to himself as he went.

Once everyone returned on board with their snacks and their drinks and their appropriate souvenir headwear, the van continued on its way.

The radio played mostly country music, because that's what the radio could pick up and no one had thought to bring any personal CDs or mp3s for travel music. They were honestly lucky that old church van's radio even worked at all.

The plan was pretty risky, but they had the right combination of powers to make it happen, assuming fate decided to smile on their mission.

Edmund had proved a tougher nut to crack than Graham. We knew his family had been under the thumb of the Superintendent, forcing Edmund to do the man's bidding.

And that was easily forgiven.

But who was he as a person?

Edmund seemed reluctant to open up. And who could blame him? He'd been a weapon of evil for months, unable to make his own life choices. But I was determined to crack that outer shell during this journey. He was nearly twenty, but he was still a kid. I didn't want him heading into adulthood with only pain and no joy or laughter.

I certainly wasn't going to press him too hard. I'd tried a few harmless questions, but he'd remained firmly in his shell for now.

The Houston crew abandoned the church van a few blocks away from the main NASA campus, which was now under the control of the DHS, like most government agencies—DHS even had offices at the post office now.

They checked into a nearby motel—two rooms—and began plans for infiltrating the space headquarters the next morning.

They would teleport in, of course, courtesy of Emmaline. No reason to risk trying to fool the gate security when you can just zap inside in a moment's notice. This would, interestingly, be Emmaline's third time breaking into a NASA structure. It had to be a record.

It was possible that these DHS jerks had a motion sensing network that could catch us sneaking in, but the odds were low and my friends figured it was worth the risk.

It was quite late and far after hours—3:13 a.m., we later pinpointed—so most of NASA's important buildings were empty save for a few overnight monitors and security guards.

"Someone near here just used their powers." It was the most Edmund had said in hours.

We had just left the Mississippi Delta and headed into the Gulf of Mexico. I turned to look at him. "What?"

"Probably less than a mile away," Edmund said. "That direction," he added, pointing in the general direction of Florida.

"Already? That's not right," I said, mostly to myself. "That's too early."

I activated the thermal vision in my implanted eyes and immediately saw that we were surrounded by boats, as a submarine broke the surface directly in front of our tiny boat.

Then lights, everywhere, bright as the sun, coming from all directions. "Turn your engine off! I repeat, turn your engine off." The voice was unremarkable, probably just a DHS coast guard captain.

I reached down and turned the key, shutting off the engine. Edmund and Graham had both moved slowly to position themselves behind me— Graham even grabbed my arm.

The submarine was small, as submarines go. It was maybe fifty feet long. It pulled up to us and moved perpendicular to our boat as the hatch opened suddenly.

Slowly a figure emerged from the sub, laughing. It was the Superintendent.

Now, I had been expecting him. Problem is, I wasn't expecting him for another day or so.

The main NASA headquarters in Houston is never completely empty. It's not like all the scientists work 9 to 5 and then go home for dinner. There are astronauts on the space station full time, which requires a crew of engineers to monitor around the clock.

Em and Bentley knew this. So the plan was never really about conceal-
ing their actions as much as it had been about not getting seen until they
pulled off what they'd come to do.

And that wouldn't be an instantaneous thing. You can't just launch a
rocket from scratch. You have to turn on and activate a hell of a lot of equipment and gear to make a rocket launch happen. And it's a process. The Ables
crew wouldn't have to wait for all the traditional checks and countdowns.
But it would take longer than a few seconds for the missile to take off.

Bentley had already verified the missile's existence via his satellite hack,
as well as the fact that it was on a launchpad in Florida, seemingly ready
to go, sitting right beside the now-empty launchpad that had been used to
destroy the moon.

But once they started things in motion here in Houston, there were still
variables. There would still likely be time for someone on the other side to
interrupt our plans or stop the launch.

So the first mission was strictly for reconnaissance. Emmaline and Patrick would enter the facility on a scouting-only mission. They would plant
cameras at Bentley's direction, as well as place devices allowing Bentley to
access the building's computer and security systems.

Then, after twenty-four hours of information gathering, they'd go in
again for the real mission of launching the missile.

By that point the kids and I would be at the actual missile launch site.

That was the moment I had been expecting the Superintendent to show up,
thinking he'd fooled me with the tracking device he injected into my bloodstream.
And by that point, the rest of the team would be zapped here by Emmaline and
strategically deployed according to Bentley's plan, along with the surprise reinforcements that Edmund's mother and sisters had hopefully rounded up by then.

But none of this went down the way we planned.

"You are pretty stupid for a smart guy," the Superintendent sneered.

He wore an all-white tuxedo—his standard outfit for a few years now,
though he sometimes mixed up the color of the tie—and he carried his

famous gold-tipped cane, though he was not known to have any significant injury or limp. I guess he just liked having it around as a prop.

In response, for now, I said nothing. But my mind was racing.

This is way too soon. They're only doing reconnaissance tonight. That missile isn't ready, and I have no reinforcements. Oh God, these kids . . . how do I stop him from taking them back? This is so bad—this is so, so bad!

"How can you be smart enough to realize you've got a tracker in you," he continued unabated, "but too stupid to realize we might have also placed a microphone on your person."

My eyes widened on their own in realization, betraying my intention of playing this scene cool.

"That's right, son," he said, noticing the change in my face. "I know about Bentley and Emmaline's plan over there in Houston. I know about the missile . . . the ratty hotel they're staying in . . . your intention to overwhelm me with reinforcements at the launch site. I know everything. All because you and your smart little friends couldn't see the forest for the trees." He laughed some more. It wasn't a sinister laugh. That's what made it so annoying. It was the laugh of an uncle who just told the same joke again that he told every Thanksgiving.

I looked at the boat radio I couldn't reach. Our mission required radio silence, so all three of us had our earpiece radios out for the sake of comfort.

I think he could see my mind racing, looking for possibilities. "I got a few hundred guns trained on you all right now. I think you're thinking about using those superpowers here maybe in this . . . situation. But you make one false twitch . . . you move one object or person with your mind . . . I will have those two teenagers with you turned into Swiss cheese in half a second. Now let's stop wasting time and you three come aboard this submarine with me. She's called *The Eradicator.*" He motioned, waving his hand toward the boat. "Come on."

Emmaline and Patrick zapped into a storage closet in Cafeteria B of the NASA complex. They both looked around and confirmed they'd arrived where they had expected to.

"Okay," Em breathed.

"Okay," Pat agreed.

From this closet they would exit into the kitchen of the cafeteria and place a micro-camera in the exterior hallway facing the Security office across the hall, and then proceed to teleport to a position one hundred feet away where the hallway turns, where another micro-camera would be placed.

But as soon as they opened the closet door they were greeted by a hundred armed DHS agents pointing guns and flashlights at them and shouting "Freeze!" in unison.

"Right now," the Superintendent continued as we carefully stepped from our boat onto the submarine, "your two friends are being captured in the NASA headquarters. The rest are surrounded at the fleabag motel and will be in our custody shortly. You, sir, are defeated." He paused and looked at his stopwatch, which had been in his tuxedo vest pocket. "Let us wait just a moment for confirmation." He giggled.

There was a short silence, but I enjoyed it. For a few seconds there were no sounds at all. No birds . . . no insects . . . even the Gulf of Mexico got quiet.

Then I saw it, out of the corner of my eye, off to the west. I didn't hear it—though my hearing is exceptional, the rocket launch happened a six-hour drive from my location.

But I saw it.

And I instantly knew it was wrong.

The second missile should have originally been programmed to intercept the moon, as the first missile had been. But that first missile had succeeded in destroying the moon. So maybe the programming had been changed—but that was a huge maybe.

My Ables team was supposed to rewrite the trajectory of the missile and send it after the two large moon chunks now nearing Earth's atmosphere to send them both off course.

But the missile I saw now off to the west was spiraling almost instantly, spinning as though out of control, and never gaining enough momentum to break out of the atmosphere. It swirled and twirled up to maybe a few thousand feet before falling instantly back to Earth and fading into the ocean.

Then I heard him laughing again, like the unfunny uncle. "That's right," he said. "It's all over." He smiled broadly before sharply saying, "Now get in the sub!"

The kids and I filed down into the submarine. It was surprisingly warm, from a decorating standpoint. There was even a carpet and a couch.

I briefly wondered about the couch. *Do they have to put the couch in the frame before they put the two halves of the sub together? Or did they bring down parts and build the couch inside the submarine?*

I shrugged it off quickly enough, considering how screwed we were.

To her credit, Emmaline was faster than anyone in the Superintendent's employ. She zapped Patrick and herself out of the NASA building directly to the hotel room across the highway. Then she managed to grab everyone there and jump away just before the DHS broke the door down.

Custodian history is spotty at best, but it should be noted that Emmaline Sallinger was one of the most gifted custodians of all time, and saved more lives than most.

She jumped them all back to the base in Canada. As everyone caught their breath and reassessed the situation, Bentley remembered my mission. "Phillip!"

"You will leave these two children alone. I don't care if I have to kill you here and now in this metal tube," I threatened.

"Ah, so brash," the Superintendent dismissed me. "I've got an NPZ over this place for now, for starters, though . . . I saw your sorry attempt at battle back in Arkansas by the river. But also . . . what makes you think I want these two anymore?"

I looked at Graham and Edmund, only to see confused fear in their eyes . . . confused fear that I could not currently resolve.

"I only wanted them to find you. You and any others that stood in the way of my moon plan." I could hear the smile of pride in his voice. "And now that is achieved. There *will* be a reckoning for humans on Earth . . . there will be a nuclear winter for folks around the globe when these moon pieces strike. And I alone am in position to capitalize. I alone am in position to lead."

He stepped toward me and leaned down face-to-face.

"I don't need these two anymore. And I can't have you using them against me. So . . ." he gestured to a nearby henchman, who turned out to be a powerful Fireballer custodian. That person melted the engine of the submarine right before our eyes.

"What are you doing?!" I yelled instinctively. "You're killing us all," I blurted as the submarine started to lilt and sway downward.

"Not all of us," he smiled again. "Gerald!" he yelled, as the second hench-man he'd brought down into the sub with him appeared at his side.

"Happy drowning," he said before pausing. "Well, you'll probably suf-focate before you drown, so . . . happy suffocating." He paused again. "That just doesn't have the same ring. Oh well." Then the Superintendent snapped his fingers just before disappearing completely with both henchmen.

The submarine continued to ride the gulf currents as it slipped slowly down to the sea floor.

I felt a panic I'd never experienced before, even as my paternal instinct drew both boys closer to me, each in one arm.

The boat creaked and sighed as it made its way gently down to the sea floor. Every noise was new to us, leaving us jumpy the whole way down.

21

THE BATTLE OF FLORIDA

Emmaline made a single phone call from the Canadian base, and she got the answers she was looking for. And then my wife became a general, turning to address her troops.

"Okay, everyone, listen up," she ultimately shouted to a very large room. "Here is what we know. My husband, Phillip Sallinger, is presumed dead, along with Graham Crittendon and Edmund Ramirez. They were sunk to the ocean floor by the man known as the Superintendent.

"This is the man who destroyed the moon, the consequences of which are upon us now. We're about to see all kinds of environmental change and oceanic disruption the likes of which you have only dreamed about. This mission is critical to the lives of all custodians, and we will have to incapacitate some folks, and even kill some others."

She sighed long and hard. "To the teens and kids among us . . . I am sorry you have to grow up so fast, and not only grow up fast, but also use your abilities to injure and harm other humans. You should have had more time on the playground. But you do not. We need you now on the battlefield."

On the bottom of the Gulf of Mexico, things looked pretty bleak. We were in a small metal tube with limited rations, and no motor. We'd been sent here to die.

The Gulf seemed angrier than it should be, but I dismissed it.

Strange and frightening noises emanated all around us.

For several minutes the three of us opined on the nature of dying at the bottom of the sea.

"I think it's heroic," Graham said more than once.

"It's just a coincidence . . . a result of many other odd decisions," Edmund countered.

Things threatened to get really boring, until I started absentmindedly snapping a coin between my two hands, something I didn't even realize I was doing until Edmund pointed it out.

"Neat trick."

I looked down as the coin landed in my left hand. I nearly laughed realizing what I had been doing without realizing it. I briefly wondered if, throughout my entire years-long run refusing to use my powers, I had still been doing this absentmindedly all along.

Then I got really confused for a moment, since I was certain we'd been told by the Superintendent that we were under an NPZ. Something at the end of my mind tugged and pulled and I couldn't let it go until finally it clicked. "That's right!" I said aloud. "Bentley did a study in college—he wrote a whole paper about it—showing how NPZ powers don't work underwater! Something about how the current movements break up the bond of the NPZ's shell."

"I mean," Edmund stated bluntly, "you are clearly using your powers right now, unless that's a trick coin."

"Ha!" I was nearly giddy. "Not a trick coin. And not a trick." I was rapidly filling with confidence and hope for our escape.

Yes, I'd struggled to use my powers earlier against the guards along the river, but I did eventually use them—that poor man.

I can *control objects with my mind,* I reminded myself. *Even long metal tube objects underwater.*

"Edmund," I said aloud suddenly, "find me the strongest power usage in the last two hours."

"Yes, sir," he replied.

"Graham," I barked out next, "your powers enhance the powers of others, correct?"

"Correct," he replied enthusiastically.

"Stand by, then, son," I said. "I'm going to need your help here in a second."

The Superintendent had lately been calling his plays from the confines of a battleship just off the coast of western Florida.

Once we had confirmation of that battleship's location, I was ready to have some fun. Some destructive and vengeful fun.

I was reasonably sure that Emmaline and Patrick would have gotten away from the DHS troops sent to arrest them. The Superintendent had made just two critical errors, and they were related: he overestimated me and the true strength of my abilities, and he woefully underestimated Emmaline and Patrick. He only sent *troops* after them—he didn't send any superpowered individuals!

The battleship, which had been renamed *The Interrogator* once it became the ship the man himself called home, was anchored just offshore, which left her position somewhat fixed.

I'll admit, the math would have gone much faster if Bentley were around, but I was plenty good at math myself. Eventually I figured the speed of the sub, the correct angle of attack, and the impact an Amplifier like Graham might have on the boat . . . and I landed on a plan.

"Let's do some damage."

Graham put his hand on my arm.

I looked at him. "Now . . . don't give me a full blast here, Graham. Don't amplify me completely."

"Okay," he said, but he seemed unsure.

"Do you know what I mean?"

"Not sure," he admitted.

"Do you ever use your powers but not the full strength?"

He wrinkled his face.

My mind immediately went to analogies. "Have you ever played golf?"

"No."

"Ever play baseball?"

"No. Not really into sports."

"Alright, never mind. How about numbers?"

He lit up. "I'm excellent with numbers!"

"Great. Then let's just think of it in terms of one to ten. A ten would be your strongest use of your power, amplifying my ability as much as you possibly can. But a one, on the other hand, would be only amplifying my powers a tiny bit. You understand?"

"Yeah, I think so."

Edmund leaned in. "You were going to go with a changeup/fastball analogy, weren't you?"

"I was," I smiled.

"Okay, Graham, let's start small. I'm going to try to move this submarine and you amplify me at a level one, okay?"

"Gotcha!" He put his thumb up.

I put out my arms and tried to grab a mental hold of the sub. It took longer than I'd care to admit, but after a minute or so, I finally locked in. "Alright," I said, my eyes closed in concentration. "I've got it. Now let's see if I can move it."

I tried to push the boat forward but it didn't budge. I opened my eyes to make sure Graham was still touching me, and he was.

"Do you want me to go up to a two or a three?"

"Not just yet. Back on the riverbend I just needed to concentrate some more. Let me try again."

I visualized the sub lurching forward a few inches, focusing every ounce of my attention on that thought, and suddenly . . . it did. It jumped forward about a foot or so, I'd guess.

The teens both cheered.

"Now you can give me a level three amplification, Graham," I smiled.

This time we lifted the sub off the floor of the sea completely, gliding it through the water for several yards. It skimmed along the sand as it returned to the floor, bouncing a bit.

"Okay, give me a four."

I pushed down against the sand and launched the sub straight up.

"Alright, now back me down to a two."

I used the reduced strength of my powers to tilt the nose of the submarine up several degrees and then turned it left until we reached the right heading.

"You guys both find something to hang on to," I instructed. "Graham, gimme a seven."

"Oh baby," he replied.

His powers were extraordinary. I could actually feel the new strength that was coming from him. And it came with the added bonus of confidence—knowledge, even, that this was going to work.

Without another word I threw my arms back behind me, then whipped both rapidly toward the front of the sub, like a possessed man trying to create the most elaborate looking hand clap in history.

And we were off.

We raced through the water with ease, faster than her engines had ever been meant to carry her. I didn't even need to use my powers anymore. Graham and I had created enough propulsion with the initial movements that the sub's trajectory was self-sustaining.

As we neared the surface, I could feel something . . . a loss of my powers! The NPZ custodian the Superintendent was using was finally able to block my abilities now that I'd gotten this close to the water's surface.

I laughed and laughed from the submarine's command center, knowing I didn't need my powers anymore for this to work, looking through the periscope as the sub launched out of the water entirely, like a breaching whale, and landed directly on the aircraft carrier, splitting it in two instantly and with a giant cacophony of scraping and crumbling noises.

The impact broke the submarine into two pieces, with one half falling back into the Gulf. The other half settled onto the smashed deck of the carrier, allowing us to walk right out of it—though onto unstable ground, to be sure.

The aircraft carrier was definitely going to sink, and soon.

Jets and helicopters were flung into the air from the impact, along with members of the boat's staff. The command tower broke at the base and fell to the aft side of the deck, which was racing up to meet it.

There were other DHS boats nearby, and plenty of land troops on the beach, so this thing was far from over. But I could feel that my powers were restored; the submarine crash must have taken out the NPZ user. That would definitely work in my favor.

I felt strong. I felt powerful and angry.

I stood, as best I could on the shaky wreckage, and defiantly gestured all around me, arms open wide, letting the entire world know that I was taking all comers right now. For the first time in a long time, I allowed myself to believe death was possible, maybe even imminent, but I simply did not care anymore. I was ready to die fighting evil like this.

The enemy responded by launching a barrage of short-range missiles at me from the beach.

I assumed they were heat-seeking, but I still used my powers to stop them mid-air, turn them around, and let them loose on whoever had sent them. Explosions popped up all along the beach.

Just then, almost on cue, there was a tremendous flash of light, and suddenly the rest of my crew arrived via Emmaline's teleportation. Winnie and Patrick set about speed-rescuing folks who'd fallen from the upended/split ship and were flailing about in the Gulf.

Henry protected a few folks from drowning by covering them with his defensive bubble; he rescued DHS people left and right, not concerned with their allegiances.

A female I didn't recognize swooped in from the air and absorbed the explosions from the next barrage of missiles, taking the energy seemingly inside her own body. She glowed for a moment, then looked at me and winked. Then she was off.

Next I saw Freddie going full-size on the shore as he began grabbing henchmen and DHS culprits left and right.

It was a battle, by the basic definition, but it was quickly becoming hilariously one-sided.

I looked toward my wife, explosions and sounds of war all around me, and signed, *"How did you do this?"*

She smiled and signed back, *"We found you with a satellite and Bentley's cunning. We've also got some new friends."*

"I can see that." I was astonished. All around me raced dozens of custodians I didn't know and had never met or heard of. Flyers, Fireballers, Teleporters, even a Telekinetic like me—everywhere I looked raced heroes capturing DHS agents and soldiers, confiscating weapons, and assisting injured personnel.

This battle was going to be over very quickly, and I had one important score to settle.

I grabbed Graham's hand and marched up the slight incline of the aft of the carrier, wreckage and fire around us, gear still sliding down past us into the water.

We marched with determination and drive, mostly from me—I doubt Graham had any idea what I was up to.

In a few minutes we reached the crashed command tower. I switched between all the fancy vision settings on my eyes, and finally the thermal vision showed me a man climbing over the broken glass of the bridge windows, trying to crawl to safety. I switched back to regular vision, but zoomed in tight.

The figure wore an all-white tuxedo, though it was long-since smudged with oil and char and blood.

The Superintendent.

I didn't feel any need to speak to the man. I had no verbal scores to settle or wrongs to right. He was clearly insane, so reasoning with him would do nothing. There was no hope that kind words of wisdom would be received or appreciated. This man was the devil in flesh. The only message I had to send could be sent nonverbally.

I leaned down and spoke to Graham face-to-face. "Graham, I'm not going to kill this man. But I'm going to hurt him. Do you have a problem being a part of that?"

Graham didn't even pause. Didn't take a moment to think or consider. Just immediately said, "Hell no."

I stood and reached out my hands, mentally feeling for and eventually finding and grabbing his form with my brain.

"Graham," I said flatly, "now you can give me the ten. Or even the eleven if you think you've got strength you've never tapped into before. Just give me all you've got, yeah?"

"Yes, sir," Graham agreed.

At that, the Superintendent began a flight that at times seemed to exceed a hundred miles per hour and sent him up to a few hundred feet into the air, and ultimately splashed him down in the middle of the Pacific Ocean. I mean I flung his ass to next Tuesday.

By the time he found land or rescue at sea, his entire regime would be demolished and replaced. The custodians had long had a ready-to-go board of humans and custodians that could handle a transition of governmental power.

I personally hoped he got eaten by sharks before ever seeing another human being again.

22

MOONFALL

Most of west-central Florida was in chaos as custodial forces arrived en masse to subdue and arrest the DHS agents and everyone in the Superintendent's regime.

We later learned that when the DHS personnel around the country found out the Superintendent had fallen as a leader, many had just quit on the spot, some burning their uniforms. I guess they assumed we would come after a lot of them to face charges for any crimes they had committed while "just following orders," and we would.

Even an iron grip on a country can be just a single event away from slipping.

Edmund's mother and sisters had made good on their promise to recruit more heroes to the cause, and then some. Everyone they knew contacted everyone they knew, and so on and so on, and there were nearly a hundred custodians in this battle. Many shone with the flourish one can only achieve via the anger at being forced into hiding for several years. Everyone had instructions not to kill indiscriminately, but to defend themselves as needed.

In Washington, even the Capitol Police were out arresting members of the Cabinet, Congress, and anyone else who had pledged allegiance to the now-deposed dictator. And that is what he was. A dictator. And he used his absolute power to attack and kill people he didn't like, mostly because he was afraid of them. It had been a bigoted administration, one aimed at the genocide of those with custodian DNA.

A single news helicopter had gotten to the site of the battle just in time to grab footage of me giving the Superintendent the old heave-ho, so the whole world knew that he and almost all his top brass were either dead or captured.

While many had felt powerless to act prior to the Battle of Florida, its outcome had emboldened the long-dormant resistance to speak up. And more importantly, to act.

Regular police and National Guard members started detaining pro-Superintendent personnel across the country. Lionel Milliken—the Chairman, the Superintendent—had only achieved power with the help of followers, and the loudest and wealthiest of those supporters were going to go to prison for a long time or slink away and hide forever.

The tide was turning fast.

The tides!

I suddenly remembered the other crisis we were facing, looking up at the two now-massive-looking moon chunks slowly barreling toward the planet.

Ooph!

"What are you thinking?" Em asked.

"I'm thinking," I began, before pausing to look down as the water continued to swallow the remains of two former sea vessels, "we'd better get off this boat before it sinks."

"Yeah," she agreed.

"Graham? Edmund?"

They both responded—thankfully Edmund had followed Graham and me as we'd walked up to the smashed command center.

"Get in here," I said, putting out my hand. "Take us . . ." I turned to Emmaline, "I guess wherever everyone else is."

Ooph!

Not a second later we were standing on a stretch of the beach about a thousand yards south of the wreckage and battle remains. There we were greeted by a dozen or so people—most of the rest of the Ables crew as well as Edmund's mother and sisters. There was much hugging, and even more weeping.

Finally, when things subsided, I looked back up at the moon.

"Do you think you can move them?" my wife asked.

"With a little help, I know I can." I confidently rolled up my sleeves and without breaking my gaze on the falling moon parts, I said, "Graham, you can dial me up to ten or eleven again . . . twelve even, if you have it in you."

"But Mr. Sall—"

I barely heard Edmund's voice before I'd already reached out with every ounce of my being along with every ounce of Graham's amplification. Whatever part of my brain heard him speaking also dismissed it as unimportant at this time. It was showtime. It was time to save the freaking world.

I crossed my arms above my head while mentally grabbing hold of each of the impending moon chunks. I paused for a deep breath. I closed my eyes to let my powers take over. Everything around me went to silence as I focused on the biggest task I would ever face.

I held my breath, then suddenly uncrossed my arms as quickly as possible, opening my hands in the process, releasing the lunar pieces with my brain.

Much to my relief, and I'm sure the relief of many others, I opened my eyes to see the two moon pieces zipping off into space, rapidly leaving Earth's orbit and eliminating the immediate danger of impact, tsunamis, earthquakes, and more.

There were still a lot of smaller pieces falling, but many would burn up in the atmosphere, and none of the rest were going to demolish more than a car or a home. No planet-killing moon asteroids were left.

A great cheer went up among the small group around me, then seconds later a much larger cheer went up from the battle site, then a chorus of cheering came at us from all around, as the residents of Western Florida learned that the threat of nuclear winter from impact of the moon was over.

I imagined fireworks would be going off, if people still had fireworks or set them off to honor certain occasions. The pockets of cheers being so spaced apart was a reminder of how many Americans had died or fled under the Superintendent's reign. Of how many entire towns and counties had been decimated in his scorched-earth campaign against custodians and those who supported them.

I was pretty relieved myself, though I wasn't quite ready to let out a happy cheer. I felt kind of tired, actually. Maybe too tired.

I looked around at the faces of my friends and family.

My wife seemed very proud, prouder than maybe was necessary.

Henry and Winnie actually looked shocked, maybe even a little . . . scared?

I looked at Bentley, standing next to his son, who was giving me a wide grin and a thumbs up. Then I turned to look at—

Wait. Graham is way over there? He didn't . . . he wasn't . . . I did that by myself?!

This was a revelation I was unprepared for. That wasn't moving a train. That wasn't moving a submarine. That was moving nearly half the moon! At the same time!

It didn't compute. I did not believe it. Because if it were true that I'd just done that on my own, it means a level of telekinetic power no one has ever dreamed of is possible.

I looked at my wife again, cocking my head. No, wait . . . I wasn't cocking my head . . . I was falling to the ground. I passed out before my head made impact on the sand.

"He's waking up!" I heard as blurry images filled the tiny openings I was able to create between my eyelids. It felt like really hard work just to get them open this far, yet I knew they were capable of so much more.

I smelled the seawater, which brought back flashes of visual memory of the battle and the fact that I was near the ocean. I remembered the ocean—no, wait, the Gulf of Mexico, which I guess is the ocean as far as a guy like me is concerned.

I tried to lift my head but was immediately restrained by . . . some kind of strap, I think.

"Why can't I move?"

A super blurry Emmaline-looking blob appeared above my face. "They're going to take you to a local hospital and check you for any issues. EKG, maybe, and MRI. It's fine, honey."

"What?" I asked before blacking out again.

Two days later I awoke in a hospital room.

I had no memory of how I got there, but I knew instantly that my body was feeling strong and rested . . . energized. Whatever had brought me to this hospital had long since been fixed or cured or bandaged. I felt amazing.

I jumped out of bed, letting any wires or tubes attached to my body just pop off as I stood. A tiny screechy alarm went off, but I was unbothered.

I put on the sweatpants and T-shirt I found on the chair next to the bed, and walked out into the hallway. I figured the family was probably hanging out in the cafeteria, where a steady supply of caffeine would be available while one waits for a relative to come out of a coma.

As I walked down the hall, emergency personnel raced by me, no doubt headed to my own room, where the EKG alarm was blaring. Thankfully I reached the elevator before they came back out of the room looking for me.

I found them exactly where I expected to, doing exactly what they should have been doing.

"So if we do nothing . . ." Emmaline stated, sounding like she was summarizing.

"We'll be fine for now, but eventually Earth's axis will tilt too much and we'll inch closer to the sun and everything on the planet will die." Bentley had a way with frightening science or math.

"I don't have confidence . . ." an unknown teenager said. I slightly recognized him as one of the new heroes helping in the Battle of Florida. Was he one of the new Telekinetics? I couldn't recall.

"Your confidence will increase from the addition of power your backup provides you," Bentley said, a smile in his voice. "Your powers will be amplified by a factor of at least five."

"We believe there's a decent chance you can pull it off," Freddie added.

"Hey, guys," I blurted, intentionally trying to surprise and interrupt them.

There was a minute or so of greetings, where everyone realized I was among them and tried to shake hands or hug or signal me a sort of hello, though my own family hung back to give others more direct access.

"Sounds like you are already making plans to deal with the whole 'no moon' thing," I said, nodding. "That's wise. Stopping the falling moon asteroids was only half the battle. What have you got so far?"

There was a long silence.

"You don't have anything?" I asked finally.

"It's not that we don't have anything," Bentley replied. "It's that you are not going to like what we have."

"What else is new?" I said, pulling up a chair and sitting down.

"I can't believe I'm going into space again," Emmaline moaned for the third time.

"If I had your powers," Bentley reminded her, "I would gladly take your place. Our mission isn't an ideal one, but rather one that takes advantage of and subverts the ideal."

"It's seconds," I repeated.

"But it's dark out there," Bentley reminded. "Definitely take lots of light sources."

"Right," I agreed.

"A headlamp, several belt-mounted flashlights, all the light you can carry."

"So you want me to teleport out into the deepest realm of our solar system," Em began slowly. As her husband, I could tell she was about to go off. "Where there is so little light I could bump into a micro-planet or planetoid body due to the low light—*but* I should bring a few flashlights with me because that will help a bunch . . . then find a small-enough-to-miss Pluto . . . fucking *touch it* . . . and then teleport myself *and a planetoid* back to this spot?"

"Well, not this spot," I said unnecessarily. "Hopefully just into the general atmosphere above Earth. Definitely not *on* Earth. That would be bad."

My wife shot me the look of death.

"That is the basic gist of the plan," Bentley concurred.

"How sure are you on these calculations?" she demanded. "I need to know this thing is near where you are sending me!"

"I'm ninety-seven percent sure," Bentley replied.

"Ninety-seven percent?! *Ninety-seven percent?!*" Emmaline was aghast. "That's worse than the pregnancy prevention rates of most contraceptives!"

"Why do you know that so easily?" I asked, not expecting or receiving an answer.

"We have more than one chance," Bentley reminded us all. "If you get out there and don't find Pluto, you just come back and we'll try again."

"Said the fisherman to the bait," Emmaline retorted.

Ooph!

Emmaline disappeared.

I knew from experience that her return would be a lot sooner than most of us were expec—

Ooph!

"Nothing. I saw nothing. I used all the lights. I looked left and right. It's so dark out there, you don't even know . . . a flashlight only reaches a couple feet in front of you." She panted.

"Well, let's try again," I said. "We can't give up now."

"Wait . . ." the voice was Greta's, one of the heroes of our last big group adventure. I wasn't even aware she was still hanging around our command center. "I have enough light, I guarantee it."

Indeed she did. Greta's ability was a strong and powerful light that incapacitated most custodians whose eyes witnessed it directly.

Strapped together via multiple belts, Greta and Emmaline finally zapped away into the edges of our solar system in search of Pluto.

We knew Greta's ability would light up enough sky for them to find the planetoid—but we weren't sure they'd have enough time to spot it, travel to it, and then travel back home.

Fortunately, they did.

We found out they succeeded about the same time we saw a sudden icy moon-thing just outside our own atmosphere.

"Holy shit!" I yelled, spotting an icy planetoid object just above the Earth's atmosphere. "They did it! They really did it!"

I stood and ran outside, along with many others.

I spotted Graham nearby and walked toward him.

"You wanna help me make this thing our new moon?" I asked with a smile.

"You . . . you did it on your own earlier, without me. You don't need me," Graham responded, head down.

"I did it earlier without you, son, but you saw what happened to me after, no? I fell into a puddle of myself, puking and panicking . . . and that was after moving only maybe a third of the moon. I need you. I can't do this without you. You were born for this, kid. Most custodians go their entire lives hoping to have a big save . . . a memorable moment of using one's powers to help others . . . to help save the world. This is it, dude. We need a new moon, and we need someone with your ability to help us put it in place. Please help us."

He finally lifted his head and smiled widely. "I'll help. But I'm going to eventually want to go to Disney World."

"Fair," I agreed. "Now touch my shirt or arm and give me a six or maybe a seven."

I felt for and quickly mentally grabbed hold of Pluto as it hung outside our atmosphere.

"Maybe even an eight," I corrected.

"Done," Graham replied.

I lifted my arms above my head and grabbed mental hold of the planetoid Pluto, slowly swinging it in a circle like a cattle rope.

Finally, after Bentley calculated the right trajectory and sent it to me, I finally let loose the icy sphere on a path that set it into an orbit around the Earth.

23

THE AFTERMATH

Our new "moon" was smaller than the old one, and therefore took up an orbit that was closer to Earth than our previous moon.

As an aside, having Pluto as our new moon did finally put an end to all discussion as to its status as a planet.

There were some adjustments to the tides and even the seasons, but a smaller-but-closer moon stand-in seemed to be doing the job so far. We'd have to take it a day at a time, and we had the confidence of thousands of newly proud custodians to tinker with it as we moved forward.

Regardless, this was better than no moon at all, everyone agreed.

The arrest of the Superintendent had been pretty swift, after all was said and done. While I'd hoped for a few days of suffering in the sea for him, he'd actually been rescued rather quickly.

The navy had teamed with the Coast Guard and had found him floating, clinging to a huge island of plastic, in the Pacific Ocean. He was malnourished and sunburnt, had broken bones due to his water impact, but otherwise would be able to stand trial.

His eventual trial moved quickly as well, relatively speaking. After a couple of weeks of witnesses and evidence, the jury spent only half a day deliberating.

The evidence was just too overwhelming.

There was no jury in America that could deny the footage they saw of him ordering the death of various custodians and other criminals solely on their skin color or DNA leanings. That's ignoring the hours of footage of him treating employees poorly, from name-calling to raised-voices and other offenses.

The media was universally upset, as they'd been hoping to drag the trial and the verdict out for weeks. Their frustration made me smile.

Warrants and subpoenas went out for the dozens of elected officials and law enforcement personnel that had actively helped the Superintendent skirt the laws and flex his power.

There were more trials and more victories. More punishments for more evil folks. On and on the hearings and court cases went, as each of the Superintendent's helpers met their fate, even one at a time.

In the short term, most things tried rapidly to return to normal. Many businesses stood to benefit from a calm and happy public, so they began to pretend like things were normal even if it would be a few more weeks until that were true.

Closed restaurants reopened. Local shops that had reduced their hours went back to a normal schedule of doing business.

The government sought to rebuild, of course, at every level.

I was courted heavily by the resistance and the groups in charge of reforming and rebuilding our systems. They wanted me to lead the entire nation. I realized that I had some natural leadership qualities . . . but I was done being a leader of anyone but my own kids. I certainly had no interest in shepherding an entire nation.

I promised to consult often, but ultimately I recommended Bentley for the job, as well as our old friend Greta, who'd come out of hiding after the Superintendent's demise and proven her heroism for all to see. In fact, they'd have made an excellent ticket together.

My own personal future lay not in politics or even business, but instead in my family. I was now reunited with my wife. My kids had recently been through ordeal after ordeal.

I just wanted to be a good husband and a good father. Maybe live long enough to be a grandfather, fingers crossed.

I was no longer swearing off using my powers. But I was retired from active superhero-ing. I just wanted to hang at home with my dog, Monster, and get to know my kin bit by bit.

I wanted to tell stories by campfire, grow my own food, and laugh with my kids around the dinner table . . . for the rest of my life.

The nightly quiz began at the usual time.

Tonight was Emmaline's turn to ask the questions as both kids and I went about picking and tending to the garden and the orchard.

"First question," Em said, super seriously, "for Winnifred."

Everyone ooh'd and aah'd.

"What . . . is your favorite color?" Emmaline finally asked.

"Oh," Winnie blurted out. "Blue! But also purple! But mostly blue! Sometimes green, though!" She smiled meekly.

"Disqualified for too many answers," Em replied, barely hiding a smile. "Henry, sir . . ."

"Yes!" he responded while harvesting lettuce from the garden.

"What is your favorite hobby?"

"Easy," he grinned, "harvesting from the garden while doing family trivia!"

We still lived on the family farm up north. Emmaline had taken to it a lot faster than I'd expected.

Of course, she insisted we socialize the kids more and take away some of the pressure I put on them to maintain the farm. But country living agreed with her more than she ever expected.

"Disqualified for lying, particularly when I know you have two next-gen video game systems in your room. Mister Sallinger," she called.

"Hit me," I replied while picking cucumbers as I went down the line.

"How much do you love me?"

I smiled, dropped my gloves and basket, and zipped myself over to her position on the back steps.

"I love you forever," I smiled before kissing her.

"Ew, gross," the kids cried.

And that was it for me.

I wish I could tell you one more tale, where, in my sixties, I come out of retirement and beat some ass. But it didn't happen.

In fact, I never properly heroed again.

Instead I changed diapers. I went to Little League games. I helped with science fair projects and attended boring graduation ceremonies.

Instead of coming out of retirement in my sixties, I was playing with my new grandchild.

It's not that there wasn't suffering in the world . . . because there was. It's not that the world didn't need heroes anymore, because they did.

But my time . . . my specific duty to humanity . . . that debt was paid.

Paid twice over.

From here forward, my path to being a hero lay solely in my ability to raise my children and spoil my grandchildren.

THE END

ABOUT THE AUTHOR

JEREMY SCOTT is the narrator behind the incredibly popular *Cinema-Sins* channel, which is home to the *Everything Wrong With, Conversations with Myself about Movies, Movie Recipes*, and *What's the Damage?* series. The channel's motto is "No movie is without sin," and it has earned more than 8 million subscribers. He co-created the *CinemaSins* brand with his partner, Chris Atkinson, whom he met while both worked as managers for a movie theater in 1999. He became a cinephile while in college, where he earned a bachelor of arts in speech communications.